Barons of the Outback

Rich, rugged...and ready to marry!

In the searing heat of Wangaree Valley, where the rainbow colors of the birds and flowers mix with the invigorating smell of the native eucalyptus, sheep barons Guy Radcliffe and Linc Mastermann work hard to be at the very top of their game. They are men of the earth, strong and powerful. Their wealth and success means Guy and Linc are two of Australia's most eligible bachelors—and now they're looking for brides!

Available now, read all about gorgeous Guy in
WEDDING AT WANGAREE VALLEY

Coming next month, Linc's story in
BRIDE AT BRIAR'S RIDGE

Guy Radcliffe was a real heartbreaker. Alana started to wonder if she'd dreamed he had proposed marriage just a few days ago.

If it wasn't a dream, what was she supposed to say? I love you very, very much, Guy, but *no.* She had always suffered from the sin of pride. He hadn't said a single word about loving *her.* Instead he had come up with a serious proposal. An *arrangement;* a *business* deal. He was, after all, a high-profile businessman, a master of strategy.

She had just about accepted he wanted her. Those kisses didn't lie. Did he count on falling in love with her eventually? Or had he seen too much of love destroying lives? She had known Guy Radcliffe all her life. Now he had asked her to marry him. Not only that, he was waiting on a response from her....

MARGARET WAY

Wedding at Wangaree Valley

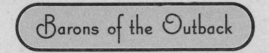

Barons of the Outback

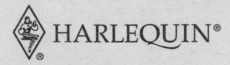

TORONTO • NEW YORK • LONDON
AMSTERDAM • PARIS • SYDNEY • HAMBURG
STOCKHOLM • ATHENS • TOKYO • MILAN • MADRID
PRAGUE • WARSAW • BUDAPEST • AUCKLAND

ISBN-13: 978-0-373-17535-2
ISBN-10:   0-373-17535-3

WEDDING AT WANGAREE VALLEY

First North American Publication 2008.

Printed in U.S.A.

Margaret Way, a definite Leo, was born and raised in the subtropical river city of Brisbane, capital of the sunshine state of Queensland. A Conservatorium-trained pianist, teacher, accompanist and vocal coach, she found her musical career came to an unexpected end when she took up writing, initially as a fun thing to do. She currently lives in a harborside apartment at beautiful Raby Bay, a thirty-minute drive from the state capital, where she loves dining *al fresco* on her plant-filled balcony, overlooking a translucent green marina filled with all manner of pleasure craft— from motor cruisers costing millions of dollars and big, graceful yachts with carved masts standing tall against the cloudless blue sky to little bay runabouts. No one and nothing is in a mad rush, so she finds the laid-back village atmosphere very conducive to her writing. With well more than one hundred books to her credit, she still believes her best is yet to come.

CHAPTER ONE

ALANA awoke before the birds. She had long since made it her habit. This was the time when the Valley was possessed of a special magic. Misty shades and depths cloaked the land, sliding down the ravines between the sentinel hills, only to vanish with the first slants of the rising sun. Occasionally a lone kookaburra beat her to it, but she managed her pre-dawn awakening pretty much every day of her life, even on Sunday, and Sunday was her well-deserved day of rest. She didn't need the hysterical wake-up call of the kookaburras or the ecstatic screech of flocks of cockatoos to rouse her. Her body clock was set. Besides, there was such beauty in the stillness, a wonderful *quietude* of the heart, that reached out and folded her in its soft arms.

Barefooted, she padded out onto the verandah, her spirits lifting as she was swept by cool little breezes. They whipped at her thin nightdress, moulding it against her body like petals sheathed a rose. She arched her back and stretched her arms, something sensual in her actions. The palest green mist hung over the densely treed hills, and the sky above was a transparent grey that was washed with pastel bands of yellow and amethyst along the horizon.

One twinkling star still blossomed, diamond-white with the faintest pink halo.

She had a wonderful unobstructed view over the Valley from the upper verandah. At all times of the day it presented a picture postcard of this part of rural Australia that was well beyond the precincts of the great Desert Heart. The garden beneath her was overflowing with colour: hibiscus, oleander, frangipani, giant bouginvillaea bushes in hot pink, purple and white. They spilled over arbours and walls and even climbed trees in their bid to reach the sun; close by, a rich diversity of nectar bearing native shrubs brought in parrots and brilliantly plumaged little lorikeets in their legions. It made a wild paradise of a garden that was now sadly neglected and in many places running rampant. The garden was huge by any standards. There simply wasn't the time.

Briar's Ridge was the centre of her life, but nowadays the homestead was hurting badly. Still, the Valley was the most desirable place on earth to live. This was where she was rooted. This was the place she had run wild as a child. She loved the fragrance of the eucalypts that dominated the high ridges, filling her lungs with their astonishing freshness. She felt she could even gargle on it, it had such antiseptic power. The eucalypts could be counted upon to flood the landscape with their marvellous aromatic scents and, when in flower, an amazing range of pods and blossom. Reluctantly she lifted her hands off the balustrade. It was *so* beautiful, a still dreaming world, but already the sky was lightening. Better get going.

Another day, another battle for survival. Over the past three years the farm had been going downhill, despite all their back-breaking hard work. Of course there was the drought. The man on the land was always fighting drought, but her father's decline into a grief-stricken, booze-fuelled lethargy was the crux of the matter. Inside she was torn by her suspicions over Guy Radcliffe—the man she privately dubbed Lord and Master of the Valley—who had been giving her father a helping hand. It was all done on the quiet, of course. That was

Guy's way. Nevertheless, the thought oppressed her. Her feelings towards Guy—though she had known him all her life—were so strangely ambivalent they filled her with confusion; a confusion she was always at great pains to hide.

Guy Radcliffe, as Master of Wangaree, one of the nation's great historic sheep stations, was without a doubt the richest and most successful man in a highly prosperous region, and he was a well-known philanthropist. It was equally well known that he liked to keep his many dealings with his adoring subjects strictly under wraps. Dispensing largesse and a helping hand was a Radcliffe tradition, as befitting the Valley's leading family since the earliest days of settlement. Guy's ancestors had pioneered Wangaree Valley. For more than a century their wealth had ridden on the sheep's back. Then, with the downturn in the wool industry, the Radcliffes had been among the first of the sheep barons to diversify. These days Radcliffe Wine Estates had been added to the family portfolio. In a few short years it was already at the forefront of viticulture, with Guy as company chairman and brilliant CEO.

There wasn't much Guy couldn't do. He was *The Man*. No argument. Not only did he oversee the Radcliffe wine and olive production, he also still adhered to the old tradition of producing the world's best ultra-fine wool, prized by the textile industry and the world's great fashion houses. This most beautiful and expensive cloth was well suited to blending with silk and cashmere. Briar's Ridge, on the other hand, had until fairly recently produced excellent fine-medium wool, suitable for middle-weight suiting. If the coming wool sales went badly, the farm could slide into ruin.

Could they possibly hold on?

A few splashes of bracingly cold water brought her fully awake. She stared in the mirror unseeingly as she patted her face dry with a soft towel. She always laid her gear out the night before to save time: same old thing. Hers was a uniform of tight fitting jeans—she looked great in them, or so her good friend Simon told her—and today a blue and white checked cotton shirt. Seated on the side of the bed, she bent to retrieve her boots, pulling them on over grey socks. She didn't even bother to check her appearance. Who was to see her but the sheep and her dogs? The dogs were beautiful border collies, Monty and Brig—Brig being short for Brigadier. Border collies were special dogs, in her opinion. Though some sheep men in the Valley wouldn't have them. They thought them too temperamental, preferring sprightly kelpies or Australian Shepherds. Certainly Border Collies could seriously misbehave if they weren't getting enough exercise. They had quite a tendency to nip heels, which didn't make them popular with visitors, and they could be destructive, but their phenomenal intelligence, their wonderful herding ability and their infinite energy, willingness and capacity to work tirelessly all day long had won Alana's heart.

From long habit she quickly applied sunblock to her face, throat and the V above her shirt, and put protective gloss over her lips. A square of scarlet silk secured her thick honey blonde hair at the nape. She shoved her well worn cream Akubra down over her forehead as she made for the door. Barely ten minutes had elapsed, but the light had changed. The soft dove-grey of pre-dawn was taking on a solid blue cast as the sun leaned over the hills, flooding the Valley in golden dayshine.

Now the dawn chorus was up, building to a great crescendo. The noise was deafening to a city-dweller. *She* loved it. Nothing sweeter. Thousands and thousands of male birds in the Valley calling love songs to the thousands and thousands of females ready to listen. It usually took a good hour for the cacophony to die down, but some birds persisted for the best part of the day, pouring out their passion.

Today it was her job to ride up into the hills and round up the wethers—the castrated male sheep—before they started to scatter all over the hillside or moved deeper into the ridges with their tall trees. Usually she had her older brother Kieran's invaluable help, but Kieran was away in Sydney on business for their dad. Briar's Ridge was so deep in hock there was the real, sickening possibility they could lose it. These days their father rarely left home. He clung to the valley where his wife, their mother, was buried. Alana swallowed on the agonisingly hard lump in her throat. She couldn't afford to break down. She was no stranger to sorrow, but life went on—no matter what.

Downstairs the homestead was silent, except for the loud ticking of the English long-case clock in the entrance hall. It kept wonderful time and was actually very valuable. Her mother had brought it and all the other beautiful antiques in the house with her on her marriage. Some people in the Valley—her Denby relatives in particular—thought Annabel Callaghan-née-Denby had married beneath her. Like the Radcliffes, the Denbys were the old squattocracy.

One hand on the mahogany banister, Alana descended the central staircase, turning left to tiptoe along the wide, polished wood corridor, covered with its splendid Persian runner—her mother's. She moved past the big master bedroom—her father no longer slept there—and on to a much smaller room that in the old days had been the nursery. There their father—a big man, easily topping six feet—had set himself up, turning his back on all his old comforts and the crushing memory of having a much loved woman lying beside him, aching to hold her when she was no longer there.

The door was ajar, so she could hear him snoring. Even that was a relief. These days, almost three years after her mother's death, Alana dreaded the thought that one morning she would find her beloved father dead. Broken hearts killed. Guilt killed. Even his drunken snoring sounded desperate. She pushed the door a little more, saw him lying, his dark, tanned, handsome face squashed into a pillow, his raven, silver-flecked curls matted. He was covered by a very beautiful ultra-fine wool rug her mother had woven. One long brown arm was flung over the side of the bed, and an empty bottle of whisky lay on its side, a few inches from his fingertips.

Just how many empty bottles had she dumped, even hidden? He always bought more. On the small bedside table was a large studio portrait in an antique silver frame. A young woman's lovely smiling face looked out of it. The hairstyle was different, but the thick honey-blonde hair, the creamy complexion, the large hazel eyes that at different times had turned pure green, were the same. Then there was the smile. It could have been a photograph of *her.* Alana vividly remembered how the close resemblance between them had delighted her mother.

"When you're older, my darling girl, you too will be named the most beautiful woman in the valley at the Naming."

The Naming was a special event at Wangaree's Wine Festival. The festival attracted large crowds from all over the State of New South Wales and beyond. Wine-lovers, food-lovers, music-lovers—they all came. And Guy always hired some famous artist to perform under the stars in the grounds of his lovely historic mansion, Wangaree. The Naming didn't happen every year, more like every three, but Guy had already announced, to great excitement, that it would be on the agenda this year. It wasn't just the honour—there was an all-inclusive holiday for two to California's beautiful Napa Valley with it, and spending money to boot!

She had no intention of entering. She thought of herself as a modest working girl. Besides, there was no money for a knock-out evening gown—though she could still get into the beautiful dress her mother had made her for her eighteenth birthday party. Let one of her Denby cousins carry off the prize. There were three of them: Violette, Lilli and Rose. All flower names, all born into a privileged world far removed from her own. Indeed, there had been little or no interaction between the families. Violette—never, *never* Vi—the eldest, at twenty-seven, and judged to be the most glamorous of the three girls, but not by much. All three sisters were extremely good-looking, although Rose was by far the nicest. Violette and Lilli were pure snobs, and Violette was one of Guy's *special friends*—but so far there had been no serious commitment, like an engagement.

Thank God! Something inside of Alana shied away violently from the thought of Violette's ever becoming Mrs Guy Radcliffe. But then she didn't want any other girl in the Valley to become his wife either. Now, that was a real puzzle. It wasn't as though she was in the running, or as if she wasted any time making herself unhappy about it. Her world was very different from Guy's. Violette was certain to win The Naming. Good luck to her.

As it happened, Alana's mother had been the inspiration for the original Naming, though the festival was the brainchild of the Radcliffes. She thought she would never be as beautiful as her mother, Annabel, and nor did she have her mother's wonderful craft skills. Her mother had excelled at quilting, rug-making, dressmaking, cooking, baking, making a house and garden beautiful, keeping her family well and happy. All those were art forms. Her mother had had them in abundance. Her own skills were with animals. Alana was an excellent rider. She had won many cross country and endurance races, beating Violette, who was a fine rider, on three separate occasions. That hadn't gone down too well with the Denbys. They had the born-to-win mentality of the Valley's social elite.

With the familiar tug of sadness she closed the door on her sleeping father, leaving him to his self induced oblivion. Every day of her life, while she was up in the hills within the cathedral of trees, she prayed he would break out of his prison of guilt and remorse. Everyone in the valley *except* Alan Callaghan knew it wasn't his fault his wife had died after a crash involving their station ute and a big four-wheel drive leisurely exploring the famous sheep and wine district. Holding to the centre of an unfamiliar valley road, the four-wheel drive had side-swiped the ute hard as it rounded a bend. Alan Callaghan and the driver of the four-wheel drive had literally walked away, with minor injuries—her father a broken wrist. Annabel Callaghan had not been so lucky. For some reason she hadn't been wearing her seat belt, though she had always been so particular with her children.

"Fasten up, Kieran. Fasten up, Lana. I don't care if we are on a back road. Do as I tell you now."

Her mother had not fastened up that day. That was the tragic part. A life lost through one careless mistake.

"I should have seen to it. Why didn't I?"

Alan Callaghan would never forgive himself.

In the big, bright yellow and white kitchen, Alana grabbed up a couple of muesli bars and an apple, then let herself out though the back door, heading for the stables. The stables were a distance from the homestead, on the far side of the home paddock. Her fastidious mother had not wanted a single horsefly to get into the house, so her father had had the stables relocated even before her mother had moved in as a new bride.

Buddy was already up and about, ready to greet her with his brilliantly white smile. Buddy, now around eighteen—no one including Buddy knew his exact age—was aboriginal, an orphan who had landed on their doorstep almost ten years ago to the day. Their mother had put the raggedy boy into a warm soapy tub, rustled up some of Alana's unisex clothes, dressed Buddy in them, then fed the starving child. Enquiries had been made, but no one had turned up to claim Buddy. The family had unofficially adopted him.

It was Buddy's job, among other tasks, to look after the

horses and keep the stables clean and orderly. He did all his jobs well and conscientiously, immensely proud of the fact that the kindly Callaghans had not only taken him in and sent him off to school—which he had loathed from day one—but eventually given him a job and, above all, somewhere nice to live.

"Morning, Miss Lana."

"Morning, Buddy." Alana returned the greeting with affection. "Hard at it, as usual?"

"I like to keep things just so. You know that. How's Mr Alan this mornin'?" Buddy loved her father. He had *worshipped* her mother. Since she'd been gone Buddy had made time to religiously look after her rose garden.

"Not so good, Buddy." Alana shook her head, fighting off a wave of despondency.

"That's real sad. Devil-man's at 'im!"

"Sure is," Alana agreed. "I'll take Cristo this morning."

"Already got 'im saddled up." Buddy gave a complacent grin. He ducked back into the cool dim interior, then returned leading a rangy bright chestnut gelding—good bloodstock, like the other five in the stable.

"You're psychic, Buddy," Alana pronounced, believing it to be so.

"Never been sick in me life, Miss Lana," Buddy protested, his expression uncertain.

"Not sick—*psychic,*" Alana answered, swinging herself up into the saddle. "Psychic means you've got spiritual powers."

"That's *me!*" Buddy visibly brightened. "Must have a teeny bit of Wangaree blood in me."

"Ah, the long-vanished Wangaree!" Alana gave a regretful sigh, looking up towards the surrounding hills.

The trees were standing tall, their silhouette greenish black against a radiant unclouded blue sky. The Valley had been the Wangaree's tribal ground. Wangaree Homestead had been named in honour of that lost tribe.

* * *

Alana toiled for hours, driving the wethers down from the ridge at a steady pace into the low country. The mustering of sheep and the directing of them to various locations around the property required plenty of patience and skill. Monty and Brig were in their element, with wonderfully eager expressions, floating around the mob and keeping them in a tidy, closely packed flowing stream. She provided the orders and her dogs carried them out, revelling in the chance to show her what they could do. A few sheep with a little more rebellion than the rest of the docile mob tried to make a break for the scrub, almost losing themselves in the golden grasses, but Monty—a low, near-invisible streak, his neck chain jingling—made quick work of herding them back into line, with a quick nip to a hapless hoof.

The creek that wound through the property was glittering, as if a crowd of people were squatting beside it flashing mirrors. Alana always wore sunglasses. They were a must to protect her eyes from the searing glare.

These wethers were due to be drenched, but she would have to wait for Kieran to help her. Kieran was due home the day after next. She missed him when he went away. Life was pretty grim and enormously worrying, with their father the way he was. It broke her heart that the less compassionate people in the district had labelled her father "the Valley drunk." Grief affected people in different ways. Her father, once a light drinker, enjoying a few cold beers at most, had embraced the whisky bottle with a vengeance.

She lifted her head to the wide-open sky. It was an incredible lapis-blue, virtually cloudless. A hot air balloon was almost directly overhead, sailing through the air as free as a bird. The Valley was a centre for sky-diving and parachuting too. She put up her hand and waved. The tourists waved back. They loved seeing the Valley this way. Wangaree and the adjoining valleys were at the very heart of one of the world's great wine growing regions, and only a few hours' drive from the country's biggest and most vibrant city: Sydney.

Mid-morning, driven by hunger, she made her way back to the homestead. Two muesli bars and an apple didn't fill a hard-working girl's tummy. She stopped for a moment to admire her mother's rose garden and say a little prayer. It was a daily ritual. She didn't know if she believed in God any more, but she did it anyway. Her mother had been a believer. She missed her mother terribly.

Alana snapped out of it with an effort. How clever Buddy was! He had taken in everything her mother had taught him. High summer, and the roses were in extravagant bloom. The colours ranged from purest white through yellows and pinks to a deep crimson. Some of her mother's favourites, the old fashioned garden roses, were wonderfully scented. Drought or no, her mother's rose garden was putting on a superb display. For that matter the drought hadn't had a detrimental effect on the grapes. The yield was down, certainly, but the quality was up. They had experienced just enough winter rain, with no damaging summer storms that could wipe out a vineyard in less than ten minutes.

She could hear Guy's well-bred, sexy voice predicting, *"This will be a vintage year."* She could hear his voice so clearly he might have been standing right beside her. But then Guy was so vitally *alive* he seemed physically present even when he wasn't. At least that was what she believed. She even had to hold back a little moan, as though something sharp pricked at her heart. In his own way Guy Radcliffe was a god, complete with a valley full of worshippers. Certainly he was as splendid as any man might wish to be. Everyone adored him.

It fell to her to be the odd woman out.

Rounding the side of the house, she saw Simon's Range Rover making its way out of the tunnel of trees that lent beauty and shade to the long drive up to the homestead. Her heart lifted.

He could stay and have something to eat with her. She and Simon were the best of friends. The bond had sprung up in pre-school. Simon had been a real dreamer then, and very, very shy. He still was, come to that, and rather a bit too much on the *intense* side. She had taken charge of him right from the beginning, almost like a little mother. Her role had been to keep Simon safe.

"You must have been put on earth just for me, Lainie!"

That had been when the two of them had been standing hand in hand before the manger at a midnight service one Christmas Eve. She had given him a big squishy hug. What a pair they must have been!

Simon had lost every playground fight when she wasn't around. The kids—and there had been some fair terrors around the Valley—had known not to mess with her. She'd been tough, and her big brother Kieran tougher. Simon was a Radcliffe—Guy's first cousin—and that should have made him bullet proof. But it hadn't—rather the reverse. Simon just seemed to be a natural-born victim. A big factor in his timidity could well have been the untimely loss of his playboy father before he was into his teens. Philip Radcliffe had died at the wheel of his high-powered car. His companion on that fateful day had not been his wife, but a Sydney socialite.

Simon's widowed mother had not gone mad with grief. She had become as bitter as ever a scorned woman could, clinging tight to Simon, her only child, and smothering him in an unhealthy possessive love. Simon, who was very bright, like all the Radcliffes, had eventually gone off to university, where he'd thought himself safe from his mother's excessive love—only to have to come home to Augusta Farm to a mother "terrified of being alone." Though anyone who saw Rebecca Radcliffe throw up her narrow dark head, flash her black eyes and flare her thin nostrils would have been forgiven for thinking she wasn't terrified of anyone or anything. It was the other way around.

Armed with an economics degree, Simon had been taken into the family firm as a matter of course. He worked on the business side of Radcliffe Wine Estates, which was now producing very high-quality chardonnay and shiraz wines. The estate's chardonnay was reaching near iconic standards. Everything Guy touched turned to gold. Another example of the rich getting richer, Alana thought. If only a bit of Guy's Midas touch could land on her father!

"It's wonderful just to see the grapes grow," Simon had once told her happily. "And Guy is the best boss in the world."

Of course he was! Guy was Simon's hero and his role model. Sometimes it put her teeth on edge, the way Simon drooled. She knew it wasn't fair of her. Guy had huge responsibilities. He took them in his stride. It was freely acknowledged that he was doing wonderful things for the Valley. Surely, then, he richly deserved everyone's devotion? There was no getting away from it. Guy Radcliffe was the driving force in Valley life. He drew people to him, men and women alike. Not that it made *her* love him the more. He didn't take any special notice of her either. Neither could she truthfully say she was invisible to him. There was something about the way he looked at her from time to time that caused moments of elation she tried hard not to show. Underneath, of course, she found Guy as impressive as everyone else. It was just that she felt compelled to keep it to herself.

"How's it going?" Simon called as he stepped out of his vehicle. As usual he had nosed it into his favourite parking spot in the shade of the lemon scented gums.

"Getting there," she answered, waiting for him to crunch across the gravel to join her.

A beautiful stone fountain was the central feature of the driveway: three tiers, topped by a life-size bronze of a little

boy. It was the work of a famous Australian sculptor—another
treasure her mother had brought with her, along with the urns
and stone statues that were dotted around the fairly extensive
garden. These days the fountain never played.

"I was about to get myself something to eat. Come and
keep me company."

"Love to." Simon showed his sweet, vulnerable smile. He
had been a delicate and sensitive little boy, and sometimes it still
showed. "Well, for a little while. I have to be getting back soon."

"How did you get off in the first place?"

They mounted the short flight of front stairs.

Simon took off his hat and threw it onto the seat of a white
wicker armchair. "I had to do a job for Guy. I was on my way
back, but I thought I'd stop in here first. You look great."

"You're an awful fool!" she laughed. "I look terrible. I'm
hot, sweating and starving."

"You *still* look great." Simon thought one of the best things
about Alana was that she either didn't know or didn't care that
her natural beauty was startling. Alana was his life. He had been
running to her for peace and comfort ever since he could
remember. "Your dad around?" His eyes slipped beyond her into
the spacious entrance hall, as though Alan Callaghan was about
to make another one of his slightly terrifying appearances.

"I guess he should be up by now," Alana said, leading the
way into the house. "Go into the kitchen while I check. You
could start the coffee if you like."

"Will do."

Simon was as familiar with the Callaghan homestead as his
own. He made his way through to the big farmhouse kitchen
at the rear. It looked out onto the summerhouse where he and
Alana had enjoyed endless after-school snacks prepared by
her lovely mother. How he had wished *he* had a mother like
that! The white lattice sides were covered in a very beautiful
climbing rose, a creamy yellow with glossy dark green

foliage, and a heavenly perfume wafted into the kitchen. He would always associate it with Annabel Callaghan. He missed her too. She had been such a radiant woman—beautiful, warm, welcoming. She and his own mother, Rebecca, could not have made a greater contrast.

Alana found her father in his study. He was dressed in knee-length khaki shorts and a clean white singlet. His heavy brown-rimmed glasses were sliding down his nose as he made his way through a fresh pile of bills.

"How are you, Dad?" Alana walked around the king-sized desk to give him a kiss.

"Awful, if you must know," he grunted, putting an arm around her waist and resting his head briefly against her shoulder.

"Your own fault." It was a mistake to give too much comfort.

"I know, but it ain't easy," he commented dryly. "The wethers have to be drenched."

Alana slumped into a leather armchair. "Unless you can help me, it will have to wait until Kieran gets home."

"Of course I'll help you," he said, just a shade testily. In her whole life Alana had never heard a harsh word from her father. "If you're up to it we'll do it this afternoon."

"If *I'm* up to it? I like that!"

"Okay, okay—I know you're a good, brave girl. The very best." He broke off as emotion threatened to overcome him.

"My heart bleeds for you, Dad," she said, very gently. After all, she didn't know what it was to love someone like her father had loved and continued to love her mother. Passion between a man and woman was a different kind of love. She hadn't experienced it as yet, and maybe she never would. Not everyone found a soul mate at will.

Alan gave himself a little mental shake. "I'm not quite the weak blubbing fool I must appear, but your mother was my shining star. She was *there* for me. In the morning she was there. When I came back at night she was there. Always shining. I still don't know what she ever saw in me, the descendant of a wicked Irish convict."

"Who was transported for the term of his natural life to Australia because he'd poached a couple of rabbits to feed his starving family," Alana said darkly. "And who by the way went on to become a well-respected pastoralist."

Her father allowed himself a smile. "Be that as it may, my Belle could have had any man in the Valley and way beyond. She could have had David Radcliffe."

For a stunned moment Alana thought she hadn't heard right. She started up in her chair, her expression aghast. *"What?"* She couldn't control her rising tone. "Guy's father?"

"The very one—God rest his soul!" Alan Callaghan, hands locked behind his head, rested back in his chair, staring up at the pressed metal ceiling.

"B-b-but—" Alana found herself stuttering now. "I've never heard a word of this." In itself this was absolutely extraordinary. "Not one word, not from anyone in the Valley— and everyone knows everyone else's business."

"Obviously they don't know it all." Her father's tone rasped as he took in her stunned expression. "It wasn't common gossip. Neither your mother nor I ever spoke about it during our marriage. I'm sure the Radcliffes didn't either—especially after David married Sidonie Bayley a few months after we married. The rebound, of course. And she's a snob like the rest of them."

"Guy isn't. Simon isn't," Alana said fairly. "But this is unbelievable, Dad." She felt immensely disturbed. "Are you saying Guy's father could have been in love with *Mum?*"

"Is that a problem?" His eyes cut to her. "I don't know why I mentioned it. It just slipped out. *Everyone* was in love with your mother, sweetheart. She was a beautiful, beautiful woman—inside and out."

"And she'll always be remembered for it." Alana tried hard

to pull herself together, but she was shocked. "Mum never made any mention of an old romance to me, and we talked about everything. That took in the Radcliffes as a matter of course. Why, she used to laugh whenever I made my little barbed comments about Guy."

"She knew you were kidding. Guy Radcliffe is a—"

"Don't tell me!" She passed a hand over her eyes. "A *prince!*"

"A real gentleman. There's your own Denby cousins, treating us like riff-raff—leave out little Rose—but I've always found Guy the most egalitarian of men. He could teach the Denbys a thing or two about courtesy and respect. His dad was the same way. No side to the man. The whole valley was devastated when Dave lost his life on the Ravenshoe site."

Alana nodded bleakly. It had been an appalling freak accident on a Radcliffe development site, when a ten-metre-high brick wall scheduled to be demolished later in the day had suddenly collapsed. David Radcliffe had been killed instantly, and his chief engineer, a short distance behind him, had narrowly escaped with significant injuries.

Alana began to wonder about certain things. "I remember coming upon Mum at the time," she confessed. "She was crying her eyes out, terribly upset. One didn't see Mum crying."

Her father took long moments to answer. "No," he rasped, and then inexplicably slammed his big hand down on a book. "David Radcliffe was a fine man, an honourable man. He left behind a fine son—a young man to be proud of. Let's leave it at that. I don't actually like talking about this, Lana. The drink loosens my tongue. I was very jealous over your mother when we were young. She was *mine.* I won her."

Was that belligerence in her father's dark blue eyes? Whatever it was, it made Alana swiftly drop the subject. "Simon is here, Dad," she said, rising to her feet. "He called in on the way back to work. Want to come and say hello? Have you had anything to eat?"

Alan shook his head. "Buddy wanted to get me breakfast earlier, but I said no. There's another good, loyal kid. I don't feel like eating, love."

"Well, you must. I insist. I'll make you a plate of sandwiches and a cup of tea."

"All right. But leave it until after Simon has left. I'll come and wave him off, but I don't want to spoil his precious time with you. He's hopelessly in love with you, poor fella. He has been for many a year."

Alana turned back at the door, her expression vaguely troubled. "Who says?"

"Me." Her father thrust a thumb at his chest.

"Well, you're wrong," she corrected him, emphatically. "Simon loves me like the sister he never had. Simon is not *in* love with me. There's a huge difference."

"Believe that, you'll believe anything," her father muttered dryly. "He's a nice boy. Always was. But he's not man enough for you, my darlin.'"

The coffee was perking by the time she walked into the kitchen. Simon had set out cups and saucers.

"I didn't know what food you were going to have…" he said.

"Just a sandwich," she said. She considered then rejected questioning Simon about any old love affair in the Radcliffe family. Better let it lie. That was certainly what her father wanted. "Have you eaten?" she asked.

"Only about an hour ago. I will have a cup of coffee, then I must be off. All set for Saturday night?"

She flashed him a reassuring smile. Simon would have been devastated had she said no. "I'm looking forward to it. So is Kieran." Her brother got on a lot better with Guy than ever she had. They were of an age, with Kieran some six months or so older.

On Saturday Guy was giving a small function at Wangaree

for visiting guests—an American couple, Chase and Amy Hartmann, members of a leading wine family in California's Napa Valley.

"Your mother's decided not to come?" she asked, striving to keep her tone non-committal. Rebecca Radcliffe's presence would put a damper on anything.

The muscles of Simon's face abruptly clenched. "Yes, and I have to say I'm glad. Sorry if it sounds disloyal, but Mum can't be relied upon to say a pleasant thing in public. It's just endless barbed comments that seem to bring all conversation to a halt. Guy only asked her because she's family and he's Guy. Lately she's taken to criticising my friendship with you."

"But she's *always* done that." Alana looked up from pouring the coffee. "Heck, she used to blame me for all the bullying that went on with those awful O'Brien boys. Oddly enough, they've turned out quite well."

"Yes—can you believe it? But Mum's jealous of anyone I care about, and you're the closest person in the world to me."

"What exactly is she worried about?" Alana was attacked by concern.

Simon directed his grey glance out of the window. "She's terrified I might get married to someone she doesn't approve of."

Alana couldn't help laughing. "Well, that just about wipes out every girl in the valley. No question of marriage for me, thanks," she added briskly. "Put her mind at rest about *me,* at least. We're best mates. Darn near brother and sister. It would be incestuous."

Looking unbearably embarrassed, Simon grasped her hand and held it. "Can't we take a step up from that, Lainie?" he begged. "No, don't pull away. You mean everything in the world to me."

She didn't have it in her to be unkind. "Well, I'm happy about that, of course. But, Simon, dear, I'm *not* your girl-friend." Gently she removed her hand. "I'm your best pal.

After The Man, Guy, of course. What's the matter with you, Simon?" she asked bracingly. The idea of making love with Simon simply wasn't on. He was very dear to her, but no— decidedly *not*. "You and I, at twenty-two, are just babies in the marital stakes. You haven't actually met a lot of girls." Almost impossible with a psychotic mother. "I thought—I rather hoped—you liked Rose?"

Glumly Simon slumped back in his chair, stirring too much sugar into his coffee. "Come on, Lainie. Rose is really sweet—unlike the terrifying Violette—and I do like her, but she's not a patch on you."

"How do you know?" Alana challenged. She had previous knowledge that her cousin Rose thought Simon equally sweet. "You have to get to know her. Rose is not only sweet and seriously pretty, she has a lot of hidden depth." Or she *could* have, Alana thought. She had a soft spot for Rose.

Simon rejected that idea. "I wouldn't care to get mixed up with that family." He actually shuddered. A gesture, she suddenly realised, very reminiscent of his mother.

"Your beloved Guy squires Violette around," she reminded him, with a little touch of malice. Or could it have been envy? "Whenever it suits him, that is." Whatever did Guy see in Violette? Apart from the fact she was stunning, always marvellously turned out and she could ride. Violette knew all about sheep farming—and wine as well. Ah, heck. Violette's assets were starting to mount up.

"Violette, like many another, is praying that one day he'll pop the question," Simon answered. "But it's not going to happen." His tone couldn't have been more positive.

"Then isn't he being rather cruel to her?" Alana asked sternly. "I can hardly believe she confided in me, but she once told me he only uses her."

"Guy most certainly isn't a user. How dare she?" Simon burst out wrathfully. "He and Violette grew up together. That's all."

"Oh, *please!*" It came out with more vehemence than Alana had intended. "Are you trying to tell me they've never been lovers?" She bit her lip, regretting her betraying outburst, though Simon—bless him—didn't appear to notice.

The very thought of Guy and Violette being lovers made her ill. There really was something weird about her feelings for Guy. On the one hand she pretended scorn; on the other hand just to catch sight of him induced the most extraordinary quickening in her body. Was it possible she was actually two people when it came to Guy Radcliffe? The Alana on the *outside* and the Alana on the *inside?*

"*Now* what deep thoughts are you thinking?" Simon startled her by asking. Mercifully he didn't wait for an answer. "Guy's no playboy, but he's no monk either. Women fall for him in droves. We all know that."

"He's too sexy for his own good."

There I go again!

"Lucky devil! I wish I had a bit of it." Simon spoke with a mix of admiration and lamentation. "But it's natural, Lainie—just like your sex appeal. You're either born with it or you aren't. Don't believe anything Violette has to tell you. She's only trying to put you off Guy, for some reason. Like I said—she's not the right woman for Guy." He put down his coffee cup, staring soulfully into Alana's eyes. "But *you* are the only girl in the world for me."

"Don't be stupid," Alana said.

Simon left soon after, leaving Alana feeling on edge and jittery. If Simon suddenly started coming over all romantic, she would have to join her father and take to the drink.

CHAPTER TWO

WANGAREE'S lovely mansion homestead stood on top of a knoll in the most beautiful part of the Valley. Everyone knew the magnificent rural property had been acquired by an Englishman, Nicholas Compton Radcliffe, in the early 1850's. Radcliffe, a man of vision and enviable private means, and set about building a homestead to rival any in the colony of New South Wales, and the style he'd chosen was Colonial Georgian. A double-storey central section dominated a serenely imposing façade flanked by one-storey wings with big handsome bays at both ends. To accommodate the hot Australian climate, canopied verandahs had been added at a later date. Rosy brick married wonderfully with the frosting of classical white pillars and beautiful white cast-iron lace. When the building had been completed it had been described in the colonial gazette of that time as "a splendid gentleman's residence."

These days only a rich family could maintain it, Alana thought, staring up the hill at the mansion. It was ablaze with lights, putting her in mind of the great liner *Queen Mary II* at night. She and Kieran had seen the ship make its majestic entry into Sydney Harbour a few months before.

They were late. She had fretted about it at first, and then she had begun to worry when Simon hadn't turned up on time. Finally he had arrived at the farm, a good forty minutes overdue. He'd looked handsome in his dinner suit, but pale and upset. It had only taken Alana a few seconds to establish why. Simon and his mother—known rather cruelly behind her back as *The Widow*—had had "words". But then Rebecca would much rather have "words" than bid her son a fond, *Goodnight, darling. Drive carefully. Have fun.*

"About what?" Alana had asked.

"Oh, let's forget it," Simon had begged, putting his arm around her and giving her an exquisitely gentle kiss.

She hadn't been able to think of a thing to say that wouldn't have sounded dreadfully impolite. It was high time Simon stood up to his mother.

Now they were going to be the last to arrive. She could see all the parked cars, among them Kieran's. He had left on his own, almost an hour before, with the wry comment, "Simon won't want *me* along as a passenger."

Did even her own brother think she and Simon were an item? Alana found herself oppressed by the idea. As fond as she was of Simon, she shrank from being so labelled. The only one on her side appeared to be Simon's mother, who always greeted her so grimly she might have been hatching some plot to snatch Simon away. Even on the odd occasion when Rebecca offered afternoon tea, she never left them alone, but stood guard.

Together, they mounted the broad sandstone steps to the pedimented portico, waiting quietly in line behind other late arriving couples to gain admittance to Wangaree's delightful entrance hall. Alana had been inside the house often enough to be familiar with it—the black and white marble floor tiles, the coffered ceiling with rosettes, the dazzling chandelier and the romantic sweep of the staircase.

There was an antique console that stood against the wall to the right of the front door, with its lovely fanlights and side lights, flanked by Chippendale chairs. She knew they were Chippendale. Guy had told her years ago when she had asked. A tall gilded mirror hung above the console, and tonight it reflected a marvellous arrangement of yellow and white liliums trailing green vines. Gilt framed watercolours of the valley had been placed precisely to either side of the antique mirror.

It suddenly struck her she really loved Wangaree homestead. She just *loved* it. There was no question Violette that would look perfectly at home there. Perhaps not *perfectly,* she consoled herself.

"You look gorgeous!" Simon mouthed reverently.

She might have been a National Treasure. "Thank you, Simon."

It was maybe the fourth time she had thanked him, but she wasn't going to knock back a compliment. She thought she looked rather gorgeous too, considering it was her eighteenth birthday party dress, halter necked, golden green, with a tiny waist and a lovely full skirt. She hadn't put on an ounce of weight. Rather she had lost a few pounds since then.

For tonight she had gone to a lot of trouble. An *incredible* lot of trouble, for her. Who was she trying to impress? Not her best mate, Simon. The results, however, were pretty good, if she said so herself. And she could rely on her hair not to let her down. Great hair, inherited from her mother. Its honey-gold thickness and shimmer gave a girl a lot of confidence.

They were moving now. Alana counted herself lucky to be invited. Did Guy think she was Simon's girl? Perhaps she should seize a moment to set him straight? Why, exactly? Would the knowledge make him rush to rearrange his life? Hardly. Simon took her arm, drawing her so tightly to him she might have been trying to make a break for it. For a minute she considered socking him—but there was the mesmerising Guy.

She had never seen a man look so intensely, magnificently *male.* Guy Radcliffe could be the archetypal hero of some heart warming romance. She thought she could safely speak for all the women of the Valley.

With that, however, came a warning.

Fall in love with him at your peril!

Wasn't she blessed that she attended that warning? She had no intention of allowing herself to fall in love with Guy Radcliffe—not even in an abstracted kind of way, like a daydream. Nevertheless, her eyes absorbed him. He looked wonderfully elegant in his evening clothes. They fitted as though they had been cut for him by a master tailor—which they probably had.

She wanted to present herself in the best possible way, but instead of the cool composure she prayed for, she felt as though she had come madly alive, and shifted up several gears.

Warily, she continued her inspection. Charisma clung to him. What an asset! His beautiful sister, Alexandra, who lived and worked in Sydney, was standing beside him to receive their guests. She too possessed the same charisma. It worked like a beacon. How extraordinarily seductive was grace and breeding! And the Radcliffes had received more than their fair share.

Alexandra was the first to greet them, Guy being caught up with a few extra words to the couple in front of them. She flashed a lovely welcoming smile, putting out her hand. Huge soulful dark eyes lit up her magnolia-skinned face. "Lana, how lovely to see you again." It wasn't just the usual thing said on such occasions. Alana could see Alex really meant it, and felt warmed by it. "And how are you, Simon?"

Simon's tanned skin pinked with pleasure. He made a funny little obeisance. "Great—just great, Alex." It was obvious Simon was in some awe of his cousins.

The two young women exchanged feather light kisses. "I'm only here for the weekend," Alexandra said, holding Alana's hands. "You must come over tomorrow and have lunch—mustn't she, Guy?"

Now the Lord of the Valley was free to give her his attention. He bent his face to her with languorous, almost regal grace.

It was the most stunning face imaginable. Alana put up a valiant struggle to meet that brilliant glance head on.

"It'd be a pleasure to have you, Alana!" he assured her, his veiled eyes moving over her.

She felt the impact of his gaze so keenly it might just as well have been his hands touching her. Part of her was ready to swoon. The weak, womanly part. Wasn't it the curse of womanhood to swoon over such men? She'd be darned if *she* would. She responded with a few graceful words of thanks.

"That's all settled, then." He smiled at her, rather ironically, she thought, but perfectly relaxed.

Oh, he had a beautiful mouth! It drew the eye irresistibly. Little brackets framed it on either side, drawing extra attention to its sexy shape. A touch ashamed, she fought down the little flares of excitement but found it a real effort. Everything about him sent a thrill through her. Her heart didn't just canter when Guy was around. It broke into a gallop. She just hoped to God he didn't know it. He had far too many female worshippers already. And a lot of them would be here tonight. She was bound to collide with her cousin, Violette. Violette had very sharp eyes.

"I want to know how life's been treating you," Alex was saying.

Alana turned to her. "I'm always kept busy, Alex." She smiled into that beautiful, poignant face.

Guy offered another comment designed to do damage. It never stopped. "May I say how beautiful you look, Alana?" He spoke in his usual smooth, self-assured way, yet she had never seen quite the type of look he was giving her. It was sort of full-on, and it provoked another chaotic flurry of sensations. She knew they were going to take a good while to settle down.

"Why, thank you, Guy!" she countered, almost as if they were sparring partners.

No use channelling your charm on me, Guy Radcliffe.

Yet his charm was drawing her into some powerful whirl-pool. She had to make a serious attempt not to be caught up in it. She knew for a certainty it would be dangerous. She didn't need Violette to tell her that.

Simon chose that moment to clamp a firm arm around her shoulders, exclaiming with great gusto, "Doesn't she just? I love the dress she's wearing. Her mother made it for her eighteenth birthday party, remember?"

Alana could have kicked her dear friend in the shins—only she saw recognition of her annoyance in Guy's amused eyes. "I do," he replied. "Your mother was very gifted, Alana."

"Indeed she was," Alex added gracefully. "I treasure the beautiful shawl she made for me."

Alana blinked back a shimmer of tears. Guy had been invited to her eighteenth birthday party. Not Alexandra. Alex had already moved to Sydney by that time. Her abrupt departure for the bright lights had come as a big shock to the Valley. Everyone had thought Alex loved her home. But Alex had left them. Alana's party had been held at the Radcliffe Estate's award winning restaurant. It had been an unforgettable night. When Guy had presented her with her present—a porcelain Art Nouveau statuette of a nymph with long golden hair—he had bent to kiss her cheek.

It had been a token birthday gesture, but she still remembered how it had felt. What could she call it? The very *essence* of sensation? It had touched every part of her, as if she was naked, even reaching down into the most intimate part of her body. She had never realised until then that a kiss on the cheek could cause such an immense erotic rush. It had been quite scary. It still was, when she thought of it—which was usually at night. Guy Radcliffe was the one person who had ever had such a galvanic effect on her. It had to be what, exactly? Fascination? Infatuation? Neither answer satisfied. It certainly didn't venture into the realm of love. As she told herself frequently, there was a lot of distance between her life and Guy's.

"Come through and meet our guests," he invited now, his dark eyes still lingering on her in that special way.

What was she supposed to do about it? She wasn't in her element flirting.

"Yes, do." Alex took her arm companionably. "The Hartmanns are lovely people. I hope you're going to enter The Naming, this year, Alana. You could win the trip to beautiful Napa Valley."

Mercifully Alex didn't add, *You could take Simon.*

The huge reception rooms swam with bright faces and happy voices. It was a smallish function—only around forty people had been invited. Alana knew them all, except for Guy's special guests, who turned out to be a delightful couple in their early thirties, good looking, outgoing, and very friendly. The wife was wearing a particularly stunning yellow chiffon dress that moulded her willowy body beautifully. Alana caught Violette studying it in detail. For once she understood Violette's avid interest in fashion. She would have loved to own a dress like that herself—especially as yellow was her colour.

"Ah, there you are, Lana," Violette said, when she encountered her. "Surely you could have risen to a new dress, dear? What *is* that, exactly? Muddy gold? Or is it muddy green? I'm sure I've seen it before." Her blue eyes bored into the lovely shot-silk taffeta of Alana's dress. "You know, you've given a whole new meaning to the word *thrifty*!"

"And you to *bitchy,* Vi, dear," Alana returned, long used to her cousin's caustic style and almost bullet-proof against it. "But I do love what *you've* got on."

It would have been too churlish not to mention it. Violette was wearing a couture strapless number in aubergine. It suited her wonderfully well. All three Denby sisters were blonde and blue eyed, but they didn't boast Alana's magnificent honey gold mane. Rose came closest, but neither she nor Lilli were present that evening. They were staying with a socialite aunt in Sydney.

Simon took her into supper, which was simply scrumptious—as expected from the restaurant's top chef, who was handling the catering. Across a table laden with delicious food, she saw Kieran talking to Alex. The really odd thing about Alex and Kieran was that, although they had known one another all their lives, these days they acted like strangers. Even now, with their eyes glued on one another, neither was smiling. Alex was tall for a woman, taller yet in silver stiletto evening shoes that matched her short glittery dress, but Kieran, at six-three, easily topped her.

Both she and Kieran took after their mother, Alana thought with nostalgia. Kieran's blond hair was swept back carelessly from his broad forehead, thick and long, like a lion's, but it suited him. His eyes, though, were their father's, an unbeliev-able blue. He wasn't wearing a dinner suit—he didn't own one—but he looked great, in a summer-weight light beige suit. She had one handsome brother, she thought with pride. And beside his goldenness, Alex's dark-haired, dark-eyed beauty looked very exotic.

Kieran had once called Alex, *"The most mysterious creature I've ever known."* Alana had thought at the time she understood. Alex had a way of looking at you, with her great lustrous, almost tragic eyes. Actually, there was something mysterious about the way her brother and Alex related to one another, Alana had often thought. Not that they met up fre-quently, living so far apart. They were both super-attractive people, but it was as if both of them had long since made the decision to walk separate paths.

Later, Alana was much in demand for dancing. Simon called her a miracle in a man's arms. Actually, it was just that she loved dancing when she got the chance. She found it as-tonishingly easy, but Simon found it extremely difficult.

"You've got to let yourself go," she advised. She really hadn't encountered anyone quite as uncoordinated as Simon on the dance floor.

"You're so brave!" he said. "If I let myself go I'd only be sorry. And so would you."

A familiar voice spoke over Alana's shoulder. "As host, it must be *my* turn."

It would be just her and Guy. So close! Instantly she felt that enormous rush. She could weep for her own susceptibility if she had the strength. Guy didn't have a loud voice, yet its special timbre, well-bred but a little edgy, sliced through the surrounding chatter.

Simon beamed at his cousin, ready to do anything he asked, and Alana spun around to face Guy, conscious of damp little tendrils of hair clinging to her cheeks and her nape. She could never look perfect when she wanted to. She knew she had a good clear skin, but it was inclined towards looking dewy instead of wonderfully matt, like Alex's or even Violette's. Perhaps her foundation was all wrong? Oh, hell—what did it matter?

Guy took her hand.

It was like being zapped. She even fancied she could see little blue arcs of static electricity crackling between her hand and his. It made her feel strangely weak—as if all her strength was draining away and her legs were about to give way. She couldn't have moved even if she had wanted to, though her heart was pounding so hard even her ears hurt. This was madness, pure and simple. It would have been much wiser to have spent the evening safely at home, tucked up with a good book.

Simon gave her a much-needed moment to collect herself. "You won't find a better dancer than Lainie in the whole valley," he told Guy fondly, only too pleased to retreat from the dance floor and leave Alana to his celebrated cousin. "You can enjoy yourself at last, Lainie," he promised, giving them a wave that looked something like a Papal benediction.

Guy couldn't help it; he laughed. "He really puts you on a pedestal, doesn't he?"

"I don't know what you mean." The time was ripe to tell him she and Simon *weren't* an item.

"Oh, nonsense!" His tone was amused, those brackets beside his mouth deepening into sensual creases.

"Maybe Simon and I should split up for a bit," she said airily. "People seem to think we're a fixture."

He drew back his dark head, staring into her eyes. "Aren't you?"

Cool. Keep cool.

So much for that! She found herself answering with intensity. "What if I dared ask if you and Violette are an item?"

"Who says we ever *were*?" he challenged.

She drew a long breath. "Most of the Valley. Simon and I aren't and never will be an item, Guy. Simon and I are best…pals. Yes—*pals* is a good word for it. I've been looking after him ever since I can remember. Certainly pre-school."

"He loves you." There was a quiet seriousness in Guy's voice.

Uncertain, she searched his eyes. They were beautiful eyes, black as night, but with a diamond sheen. "You sound serious?"

"I'm always serious with you, Alana."

Heat swept her like a flame. She could feel the flush spread out all over her body. "Well, I never knew *that!* In fact, it's a bit too much to take in. Generally you speak to me as though I haven't made much progress since my eighteenth birthday."

"A bad habit I picked up," he rejoined suavely.

"So you admit it?"

"Absolutely. You didn't *really* want me to treat you like an alluring woman, did you?"

She nearly folded, deeply surprised. "Hey, I'm not the alluring one. *You* are." The heat off her body could be throwing off sparks.

"Alana, that's plain crazy!" He spun her then, in what felt

like some elegant choreographed step. In fact the two of them were beginning to look like ballroom champions, she thought, aware people were looking their way, expressions openly admiring. "*Men* aren't alluring," he scoffed gently.

"Aren't they?" He gave off male allure in metre-high waves. "You should try reading some of Vi's romances."

"Violette reads romances? How delicious!"

As was his laugh. "Well, she might, for all I know. I was having a little joke. But, just so there's no misunderstanding, I want to make it perfectly plain. Simon and I have no plans that involve romance."

That little smile was tugging at his mouth. "Does one have to plan it?' he asked. "Surely it just happens? You wake up one morning wishing you could reach out for that special someone."

Her body quickened. She knew his hands would be just lovely. "Well, you must have done a fair bit of that—" There was the faintest trace of hostility in her voice. She broke off, horrified. He *was* her host.

He drew back to stare down at her. "It might be a good time to tell you, Ms Callaghan, that you've just about used up all my gentler feelings towards you."

"So I should start to worry?" she challenged.

For answer he pulled her in so close that the room around them started to blur.

"It might be an idea," he cautioned.

"Does that mean you can say and do what you like, but I can't?"

He didn't answer.

Silence had never seemed to say so much.

"Who would *you* reach for, Guy?" The words simply came.

"I won't terrify you and say *you*."

She, so wonderfully sure on her feet, stumbled. "You're terrifying me just thinking about it. You're joking—aren't you?"

He saw the bright confusion in her lustrous eyes. "Of

course." His glance remained on her. It brushed her face and her throat, and her very feminine creamy shoulders. "But who could blame a man for wanting you near him, Alana?"

Every single nerve-ending in her body was wired. "You're taking me somewhere, Guy," she said, unable to control the tremble in her voice. "Where is it?"

"The big question is, do you *want* to come?" His handsome face was unusually intent.

"And leave my safe little world?" she asked shakily. She marvelled at the difference in him—in her. What had changed things so dramatically? Was this precarious kind of intimacy better or was she about to jeopardise her whole future? "It would be far too easy to fall under your spell, Guy," she said. "The result could be a lot of pain." Her sharp-talking, supremely self-confident cousin hid a lot of pain.

"And you're scared of that?"

"Absolutely." She released a pent-up breath.

"So what is it about me that scares you? You certainly haven't given that impression over the years."

"You've never invited me to come close."

"You were too young. Come closer now." He gathered her in. "You're a beautiful dancer, by the way."

"Have you just noticed?"

"I've always noticed."

"You could have asked me to dance with you hundreds of times over the last couple of years, but you never have."

"In the space of a few minutes the intervening years have disappeared. Maybe I thought you were being faithful to Simon?"

Her body abandoned all pretence, trembling in his arms. "Maybe I thought you were being faithful to Violette? Among others." She couldn't resist the little waspish sting in the tail.

His hand at her back exerted a little more pressure. "Remember what I said about being more careful?"

"Actually, I remember an astonishing number of things

you've said to me," she found herself admitting. "At my eighteenth birthday party you told me I was sweet. And smart."

He gave her a disturbing smile. "Sweet, smart, and *tart*. Let's see—I remember now. I could have added passionate, argumentative, with a good sense of humour and sexy but innocent too. Sad, beautiful, a wonderful daughter and sister. The best woman rider in the valley, and that's saying something. I've always loved to see you competing. Poor Violette was always doomed to run second. Come to that, I love to see you working those Border Collies of yours. Not easy working dogs, but you instinctively know how to get the best out of them. You have a very attractive voice too. I've heard you singing to your own guitar accompaniment."

She was totally disarmed. "Now you're using your fabled charm on me, Guy."

"Is it working?" He flicked her a downward glance.

"I'm not sure it would be wise to tell you." She shook back her honey-blonde mane. "I feel sure you're pledged elsewhere. Or you soon will be."

Another couple whirled by, coming in too close. Instantly Guy's arms drew her out of harm's way.

Harm's way? Her heart rate had risen as though she had run halfway up Mount Everest. They had known each other such a very long time, but she couldn't imagine anyone who seemed so familiar yet so *new* to her. Her body fitted his so perfectly, it was beyond explanation. So perfectly she wondered if she should back off. All it needed was one tiny step over the dividing line. And there *was* a dividing line. She could never allow herself to forget that.

For the first time her graceful body offered resistance. "Cousin Vi's over there, looking like she wants to bury a tiny hatchet in my head." She tried to turn what must have been her perceptible withdrawal into a joke.

"I wouldn't let her."

Her breath shortened at his tone. "She could catch me on my own. Batter me in my sleep. Are you trying to make her jealous?" Did that explain his newfound manner?

"Don't be ridiculous." His reply was short. "I can't even see her. *You're* so dazzling."

She had a sensation she was floating. What was he trying to do to her? And why? There were so many unanswered questions spinning around in her head. "I'm dazzling all of a sudden?" she questioned, lifting sceptical eyes no longer hazel but pure green.

"Let's just say you've been dazzling me for quite a long time—though, very modestly, you've appeared unaware of it."

Modesty didn't prevent a highly explosive recklessness surging into her. Whatever it was that was happening between them, it was moving way too fast. Mistakes carried penalties, she reminded herself. "Who *are* you tonight, Guy?" She tipped her head back, to ask, "Do I really know you?"

"I don't think you do."

His voice held the faintest rasp to it, yet it was very seductive. His evident experience made her acutely conscious of her own lack of it. She was still a virgin, probably the last one left in the Valley, but that had never mattered to her. To date she hadn't met anyone she had wanted to enter into a serious love affair with. She hadn't even glimpsed anyone who didn't pale before Guy Radcliffe. Now she was discovering there was a lot of emotion locked up in her. Passion. Desperate hunger. She didn't want to feel this vulnerable. Up until now she had been rock solid, in control. A *whole* person, not part of someone else. Falling madly in love didn't guarantee happiness. Love could be abruptly withdrawn, leaving the rejected one to battle the pain.

"Wait." She placed a shaky hand against the snowy-white of his dress shirt

Immediately his expression turned to concern. "What is it?"

"Nothing really. I just feel a little odd." Her emotions, of course, were getting too hard to handle. But she couldn't tell him that.

"Let's go out onto the terrace. Get some air." His hand moved beneath her elbow guiding her outside.

The mingled scents from the garden were like incense on the warm air. Couples were standing laughing, talking, on the lush sweeping lawn; others were wandering the many stone paths, one with a little bridge that spanned a man-made pond where black swans sailed majestically and came at your call. The way was lit by hundreds and hundreds of twinkling white lights that had been placed in the density of the overhead trees.

The night was all around them, the vast dome of the sky thickly studded with glittering stars. There was Orion, the mighty hunter with his jewelled belt. The Southern Cross was so bright she understood perfectly why the aborigines worshipped it, and the Milky Way was a broad sparkling stream, the resting place of the great tribal heros.

Thoughtfully Guy produced a handkerchief to dust off the wide surrounds of a stone pillar—one of eight that supported the roof of the loggia. "Sit here. There's a lovely breeze."

"How good it feels!" she sighed, letting the breeze slide over her to cool her heated skin. Hadn't her inner voice always warned her it would be dangerous to get too close to Guy Radcliffe? And with good reason. Now that she had done so, however lightly, she realised she couldn't go back. His magic had already worked its way into her. She should do something to counteract it. But what?

He stood with his tall elegant body eased back against the pillar, looking down at her. "You're very like your mother," he told her quietly. "She was such a radiant woman. The Valley isn't as bright without her."

The gentleness and the compassion in his voice overwhelmed her. She was so incredibly touched she feared she might burst into tears. She remembered how her mother had always laughed merrily when Alana had made her tart little comments about Guy Radcliffe, Lord of the Valley. Of course her mother, skilled at recognising the truth of it, had seen through her. Now she thought there was a possibility Guy might tell her what she had so recently learned about her mother and his father. She desperately wanted to know.

Had they once had a relationship? Even a brief flutter that had burnt itself out? She had always felt a decided resistance to her from Guy's mother, Sidonie. Not that Mrs Radcliffe, who lived near Alex these days, wasn't always gracious. But she was ultra-*reserved,* withholding any real warmth.

"Guy?" She lifted her head to him, her voice betraying strong emotion.

He looked down on her. The exterior lights were making a glory of her beautiful hair, and burnishing the golden-green of her evening dress, its long skirt pooling around her. "If it's what I think you're going to ask, the answer is *no!*"

She felt the powerful rejection. "You can read my mind?"

"This time I can. You forget, I've known you since you were a little girl. I've a pretty good idea where you're heading. You were bound to hear something from your father at some point."

"And so I have—just a comment. I want *you* to tell me." She shifted position so she could look directly at him.

For a fraught moment he seemed to consider. "Alana, you shouldn't listen to gossip," he said finally.

"Gossip?" The tightness that had gathered in her throat was reflected in her voice. "There's always gossip in the Valley, but my father never gossips. I've never heard this before."

"And you're not going to hear it from me."

He said it so decisively it had the power and authority to stop her in her tracks. She rose to her feet, not knowing how to continue.

"Is that a warning?"

"No, of course not!" His brooding expression almost immediately lightened. "I'm simply stating my feelings. Leave it, Alana, please. There's nothing to be gained. Tell me how you feel now."

Rocked to my soul!

Her old self seemed to have disappeared for ever. "Much better," she lied.

The playful breeze sent a long golden strand of hair flying across her cheek. Guy reached out to smooth it back, his fingers making contact with her skin, electrifying it.

She inhaled sharply.

"Alana," he said, his hand slipping to the nape of her neck.

The depth of feeling in his voice dazed her. For a crazy minute she thought something cataclysmic was about to happen, something that would change her life. Was he going to draw her into his arms? Was he going to kiss her? Kiss her in front of all these people? Unbelievably, it felt like it. Her feelings were rubbed raw. She had a sudden overpowering urge to lift her mouth to him, but instead she moved back, the flutter in her voice betraying her state of agitation. "What am I getting myself into, Guy?" she whispered.

His answer was equally quiet and equally intense. "I guess it's about time to find out."

"You'll have to tell me what you mean." Her voice was charged with tension.

"Just let yourself go with it," he said, in a near-hypnotic voice.

Neither of them was moving. They were standing perfectly still, staring at one another; two people who were finally admitting they were powerfully drawn to each other. Alana felt her mind and body beginning to reel. She wanted to lie down. With *him*. She wanted his arms around her. Some part of her had always been tamped down. Now it was breaking out. Or trying to. She could feel it beating strongly against her ribcage. The safe option was to break the link—only she wanted whatever it was between them to bind them closer together. The ambivalence that had been in her was no more than a defence. How long had she expected to hide behind those defences? She knew they wouldn't protect her anyway.

"Are you trying to hypnotise me?" The tension in her voice betrayed the emotional storm that was in her.

"I think you *could* be hypnotised," he said gently. "Are you brave enough to let me?"

"I don't think I'm ready…"

"Some part of you has always fought me."

"I can't deny it."

He smiled. "But it hasn't lasted. Are you going to enter The Naming?"

She dropped her head. "I like to keep a low profile. You know that. Besides, the competition is fierce. It's not fair that Alex has never been able to enter."

"Alex is family," he explained. 'Besides, she doesn't need a prize trip."

"But Alana Callaghan does?" She couldn't prevent the flare of resentment.

"All I meant is, you ought to do something different, Alana. Win a trip overseas. Enjoy yourself."

She didn't look at him.She turned her luminous head away, unaware that even in the semi-dark it glowed. " I couldn't enter even if I wanted to. I couldn't take up any prize even if I won—which is a long way from certain. I'm a working girl. I have to be around to give Dad and Kieran a hand. I have to keep my eye on Dad."

"How is he?"

Although his voice was full of real interest and concern, she was immediately on the defensive. Guy was a man of immense kindness, who did things for people without drawing attention to it, but she didn't want to talk about her father, burdened for so long with the worry, the hurt and humiliation of what he had become.

"You know darn well how he is, Guy," she said, soft vehemence covering her compulsion to cry. "Dad's a mess."

"Don't! I didn't mean to upset you. I'm sorry." His hand shot out to encircle her wrist.

She didn't have the strength to pull away. This man touched her in every way. "I'm not going to embarrass you!" Her pretty teeth were gritted. The light caught the sparkle of tears.

"Do I look like I'm embarrassed?" he challenged.

On the contrary, he radiated a richly sensual tenderness.

"I'm not *ever* going to cry in front of you," she vowed.

"You'll have to take the consequences if you do," he said enigmatically, not releasing her hand, but stroking her palm with his thumb.

She swallowed hard. *Consequences?*

"Your father has always resisted grief counselling." There was regret in his voice. "That's a pity. There are very good people who can help him. One in particular I'd like him to at least meet."

She bit her lip. "He won't do it, Guy."

"What if I talk to him one more time?"

She made a sad little face. "Dad thinks the world of you, Guy. And I have an awful suspicion you've been helping us out financially, but I know you won't tell me. Even so, I don't think your trying would do any good. Kieran and I have had to give up. Dad can be very stubborn. Sometimes I think he has a death wish."

Guy's hand tightened over hers, causing her to close her eyes at the mounting excitement.

"Don't say that," he told her quickly. "There's been enough tragedy."

How could she feel comforted and yet delirious with excitement at the same time? It was a fantasy. Did he know what it was doing to her, his thumb on her hand, skin on skin?

"My mother was tremendously upset when your father was killed." Once again she had strayed into dangerous territory. "When I think back, it was like something deeply personal."

"Your mother was a truly beautiful and compassionate woman. Leave it at that, Alana." His striking features were taut.

"I wasn't… Of course I wasn't… I wouldn't dream of…"

A disdainful drawl came out of the shadows, causing them to break apart.

"So there you are, Lana," Violette called. "Simon is looking everywhere for you."

"Why? Is there some emergency?" Guy turned his dark head as Violette, emanating a powerful jealousy, stalked up to them.

She gave Guy a playful smile. "Why, Guy, you know Simon can't let her out of his sight for a minute. He's mad about the girl. Goodness, they already *look* married. And I'm not the only one to think so."

"You *are* the busy little bee, spreading all these rumours," he pointed out dryly.

"Darling!" Violette protesting took his arm. "I think it's cute. Those two have been sweethearts almost from the cradle."

A scream felt like an appropriate response to Alana. Instead she found a smile. "Pardon me if I just run along."

Once she was inside the house, Simon dived back to her side. "How did the dance go?" he asked eagerly. "You and Guy were really, really good. Everyone was watching you."

"I loved it," she confirmed, in a massive understatement. "But actually I crave a cold drink."

"There's champagne," Simon suggested, smiling helpfully. 'It's really flowing."

"Cold water would do nicely."

"I'll get some. What about club soda?'

"Fine." She nodded her head.

"There's not a thing Guy can't do." Simon, his voice full of admiration, steered her towards the drinks table

"He's The Man, all right!" she agreed laconically.

"He sure is. Look, do you suppose we could get out of here soon? It's a lovely event, but I'm not much good with parties. I soon run out of chit-chat."

"You want to go?" Alana looked around for her brother. She spotted him, yet again with Alex.

They obviously preferred talking to dancing, and it was no trivial chit-chat either. They might have been about to face a firing squad together. Another mystery there. She hadn't seen them dancing together all night. But what perfect foils they were for each other! She supposed that might equally well apply to her and Guy. The striking difference in colouring, of course, the gold and the ebony. She had a presentiment that she should follow Kieran's direction and take a separate path from the Radcliffes. It wouldn't have escaped her so-proud brother's attention that Alex was an heiress. It pretty well put a sign around her neck that read, *strictly off-limits*. Besides, when Alex was at home she was never without Roger Westcott in tow. A lot of people thought *they* would marry. The Westcotts were old squattocracy. It was the same old story. Money married money. People with a position in society married their own kind. It helped keep the family fortunes intact.

"Look, I'll stay if you want to," Simon was saying self-lessly, though he didn't really enjoy himself when Alana wasn't around. And all the fellows he knew were looking their way, no doubt awaiting an opportunity to dance with her. "You're so good with people. I envy you. I always get the feeling people don't know what I'm saying. The only person in the world I can really relax with is you."

Sadly, it was true. Rebecca's brand of mothering had had a disastrous effect on him. Simon had made reticence an art form.

"And I worship Guy," he tacked on, quite unnecessarily.

"Simon, dear, I don't have the slightest doubt of that!" She wondered for the first time in her life if she didn't worship Guy herself?

"Yet I always feel I should recharge the batteries when I'm around him. He's so vital, so focused. And Alex is a lovely person, but I don't really know her—she's so deep. Kieran always gives me the impression he'd like to see me do a stint in the army. Little Rose, now, is sweet. I can see a little bit of *you* in her."

Here was an opportunity. Alana seized it. "Well, isn't that what I keep telling you? You have to get to know Rose better."

"Let's go. Let's get out of here," Simon said by way of an answer.

When they arrived at Briar's Ridge, Simon, very properly, got out of the Range Rover to escort her to the door. "I won't see you tomorrow if you're going to Wangaree for lunch. You could come over for tea?" he suggested, giving her a beseeching look.

"Doesn't your mother require a month's notice?" Alana put up a hand and pinched his cheek, something she'd been doing since the First Grade.

"What about fish and chips down by the river?"

"My very favourite place! Down by the river it is."

She reached up to kiss his cheek, before sending him on his way, only Simon decided it was his moment to act. The light of battle was in his sky-blue eyes.

"Simon!" she gave a warning wail, not wanting to hurt him, her dearest friend, yet at the same time possessed of a fierce urge to push him away.

But Simon wasn't about to be put off. He was all buoyed up. "Lainie, I love you," he declared. "I'll kill myself if you don't let me kiss you. You're the most beautiful girl in the entire world!" He was almost choking with emotion. "Please...

please…a proper goodnight kiss." He placed his hands on her shoulders—she could feel his arms trembling as he gripped her—and dipped his dark head.

What followed was actually quite sweet. In fact Alana nearly thanked him. She'd had a lot of kisses worse than Simon's. He could easily find a girl to love him, she thought, but no way were *they* on the cusp of a grand passion.

"I think I hear Dad," she whispered, thinking that was a sure-fire way to get Simon mobile. Simon was marginally terrified of her father.

"I'd better go, then," Simon whispered back. "Promise me I'll see you tomorrow."

"I'll ring you." Inside the darkened house there was a noise, as if something fairly light had toppled over. Alana latched on to it. "Could be Dad!" she warned, knowing full well it was most likely their cat.

"Night, then!" Simon took off down the short flight of front steps, then broke into a run.

CHAPTER THREE

Briar's Ridge was into its first week of shearing. For most of the preceding week the brunt of getting the barracks ready for the shearing team had fallen on Alana. The men brought their own cook, and there was a kitchen, bathrooms, and a large communal shower room, but it all had to be cleaned, swept and dusted, mattresses aired, then beds made up with fresh sheets. Alana had had to dig deep to get through it all, but the last sheep was expected to be shorn by the end of the following week.

Wangaree, by far the biggest property in the valley, was already underway, with its shearing expected to go on for weeks.

Alana had loved shearing time from when she was a little girl, and the itinerant shearers—all regulars to Briar's Ridge—had made a little mascot of her. An extra bonus for this week was the gratifying way her father had managed to remain sober and on the job.

When Alana wasn't droving sheep to the shed, or taking shorn sheep back to the paddocks, part of her time was spent with the shearers—much to the delight of the men, in particular a newcomer to their ranks, with an excellent reference from a big Western Queensland station.

Even dressed in unisex jeans and a cotton shirt, there was no mistaking Alana for anything else but a beautiful, vibrant young woman with a powerful sex appeal that was entirely natural. Admiring glances came her way aplenty, but no man was fool enough to look at her directly with lust in his eyes. Alan Callaghan was still a daunting presence in the sheds and around the yards. There was her brother Kieran too, a great bloke, but fiercely protective of his sister. And then there were Alana's dogs, a formidable pair. The upshot was that Alana went where she pleased without a moment's hassle.

Apart from her golden beauty, the men admired her for her proven abilities and capacity for hard work. Alana could shear a sheep with the best of them. Maybe she didn't have their strength and endurance, and she couldn't keep up the count or the pace—she was a woman after all, very fit and in splendid shape but at the end of the day no match for a man—but she came into her own instructing her dogs to draft the sheep through the yards. It was fascinating to watch the dogs in action. Up, under, around, running along the sheeps' backs. In the shed Alana worked hard, picking up the shorn white fleece the instant it was ready, then throwing it in a smooth arc onto a long slatted table.

That particular day when the men were more than ready for their mid-morning break—although there were no smokers any more, like in the old days, no pollution of human lungs let alone the wool—Thommo, their best and fastest shearer, even if he was the oldest, let her have a go finishing off the last sheep. Thommo had given her and Kieran lots of tips about shearing over the years, which they had taken on board.

"Come on, love. Your go," Thommo said encouragingly.

"Thanks, Thommo." There was still plenty to learn.

Beneath her blue shirt Alana was wearing a sports bra and a yellow singlet. All the exterior doors and windows were open, but it had grown very hot in the shed. Without a thought, unselfconsciously she ripped off her cotton shirt.

"Sheep-o!" Thommo yelled as he pulled a fairly hefty ewe from the pen. "You're on the clock, love."

And this, then, was how Kieran and Guy found her, when they walked down to the shed to check on how the wool was coming.

"Well under four minutes!" Thommo congratulated her, well pleased.

He took a closer look. She had freed the wool cleanly in one piece, nice and close to the loose kinky skin. He threw her a clean towel and she moved forward to catch it. Sweat was running down the side of her face from her temples, trickling into her cleavage. She was positively *glowing*.

Guy gave no indication of it, but he was deeply rattled. This wasn't the Alana he had seen a few weeks back, at the party for the Hartmanns. She had been so beautiful then, in her golden-green dress, hair and make-up immaculate. This was the tomboy Alana Callaghan Guy remembered from only a handful of years before, but the luminosity she had inherited from her mother was a thousand times more potent. She didn't seem at all uncomfortable, yet the tight yellow singlet drew attention to her small, beautifully shaped breasts, her taut midriff, tiny waist, and the slender strength of her arms. Her lovely, glossier-than-satin skin was dewed with sweat, the ponytail at her nape a damp honey-gold tangle.

She looked incredibly erotic.

Guy felt a hard knot tightening in his chest. He felt a powerful impulse to strip off his own shirt and cover her up. His eyes whipped around the shed. Most of the men he knew. They were regulars on the circuit. One fellow he didn't: young, heavy build, heavy wrists and shoulders, good-looking in a rough sort of way, dark overnight growth on his face. *His* response to Alana was showing only too starkly.

Guy found himself jamming his hands so they came together like fists. He loathed violence. He'd never had to employ it—he knew he commanded a lot of respect that pre-cluded it—but he had a driving urge to run the shearer not only out of the shed but off a property that wasn't even his. He had to force himself to calm. If he had *his* way, Alana would be barred from the shed.

His sister Alex had been treated like a princess from birth. *Alex* had never been allowed to wander at will around the shearing sheds when the men were there working. *She* certainly didn't know how to shear a sheep and class the wool, much less work energetic sheep dogs. Alex's place had been at the homestead with their mother. She had gone on to university, after which, armed with an arts degree majoring in Fine Art, she had been offered a job at arguably the best art gallery in the country, owned and run by a family friend. A smooth ride—as Alex would be the first one to admit.

Alana too had had her chance at university, but when her mother had been killed there had been nothing else for it but for her to come home. For the past three years she had been a full-time, hard-working farm girl, coping valiantly with a guilt-ridden father with a potentially fatal drinking problem. No easy life for a twenty-two-year-old girl. It came to Guy, not for the first time, that *he* was powerfully protective of her.

The shearers' cook, a wiry little Chinese man, entered a side door, calling out, "Smoko!" to the men. Morning tea was ready, which meant a mountain of sandwiches, fresh dampers with butter, golden honey or strawberry jam, and a gallon of billy tea.

As she towelled herself off, Alana caught sight of the two men in the main doorway. Their tall, lean figures, wide in the shoulders, narrow in the hips, were silhouetted against the brilliant sunlight.

Guy! He had only to appear and she came unstuck. Settle down, her inner voice advised. She shouldn't let him do this to her, but so much of life just *happened.*

Totally unselfconscious only a few minutes before, now

she threw the towel down and made a hasty grab for her shirt, pulling it on but letting it hang loose.

"Hey, Lana—want to organise some morning tea for us?" Kieran called to her in a cajoling voice. "I'll have a few words with Thommo, then I'll join you both back at the house. Don't worry about Dad. He and Buddy are flat out at the Second Paddock."

"Fine. I'll wash up first." She walked towards Guy, while Kieran followed the shearers outside into the sunlit courtyard.

"Morning, Guy," she managed brightly, although her throat had gone bone-dry. "This is a surprise." She led him off on the shortest route to the house.

Brilliantly enamelled parrots squawked overhead; and a fresh gust of wind sent spent petals flying from the seductive smelling flowers.

"I wanted to have a word with your father."

"Oh?" She looked up at him quickly, trying to decipher what lay behind those fathomless dark eyes. He sounded very distant for Guy. Indeed, he looked daunting. His eyes were clouded—but with what? Some strong feeling, that was for sure. It unnerved her. Was it anger that overwhelmed him? If so, about what? She kept her head tilted towards him, feeling enormously heated—and it wasn't just from her recent physical activity. Emotions were running dangerously high. She had never seen Guy this way. She tried to cover her inner agitation with whatever veneer she could muster. "What about?"

"We want to keep it to ourselves." His expression lightened, but it still troubled her.

"Now you've got me really interested."

"While keeping you out of the loop?" He gave her a faint sideways smile. "No, it's just private stuff, Alana. Nothing to worry or concern you." His glance swept her, increasing her jitters.

She was wearing some light gloss that made her heart-shaped mouth look moist and luscious, Guy thought. He knew there were many young men in the Valley in love with her, his own cousin included, but she wasn't looking to get rescued from the farm. She loved Briar's Ridge. She was a true country girl, but just too damned desirable to work with the men.

"Shearing is gruelling work," he said, hearing it come out a lot more tersely than he'd intended.

"You mean you don't approve of my taking part?" She stared up at him with a little questioning frown. His attitude had taken her by surprise.

He was silent a moment. "Actually, I don't. There's a new fellow on the team. What's his name?"

She gave a little laugh. "Gosh, you worked that out pretty fast. He's a New Zealander, and he's good. Great co-ordination. I can't remember his name. I think it's Dean."

"Then *Dean* had better keep his eyes off you."

It was preposterous. He was *jealous*. "I never thought you so arrogant, Guy Radcliffe!"

His mouth compressed. "It's not that I'm arrogant. To put it simply, I'm older and wiser than you."

"Oh, yes! You're my superior in every way."

"At various times I might be. You should consider keeping your shirt on around the men."

She made a sound of intense irritation. "What a sensible suggestion! You're really jealous, huh?"

He shrugged a shoulder. "No, just concerned. Your father and Kieran can't keep their eye on you all the time."

Alana could feel her temper go from simmer to boil. "Gee, Guy, it's so nice you called in. Don't you think I can look after myself?"

"Sorry, Alana. You can—better than most. But I wouldn't like to see anyone bothering you."

"What would you do?" she challenged, thinking that the elegant Guy Radcliffe, who never raised his voice, wouldn't be the man to cross. At that very moment the Lord of the Valley looked mighty tough.

He held a bougainvillaea bough freighted with hot pink blossom away from her head. "You've seen me cracking a whip haven't you?" he asked. Whips were used by stockmen to assist in the mustering process. Alana knew better than most that it wasn't anywhere as easy as it looked. Guy was wonderful to watch.

"I've got a big brother, Guy," she pointed out sweetly.

"I don't feel in the least brotherly."

It took a full minute for her to respond. "How about cousinly?" she suggested.

"Not even close. Kieran is enormously protective of you, and he worries when he has to go away."

It was the truth. "You Valley men are all so old fashioned. Don't deny it. You are."

He surprised her by coming to a halt, then turning her towards him. "Men have always been attracted to beautiful women, Alana. Most are civilised and keep their admiration within prescribed bounds. *Some* don't."

Her hazel eyes sparkled as she lifted her chin. "You sound like you want to sack my new man on the spot?"

"I'm going on instinct." His dark gaze was very serious.

"What was he doing?" She broke away angrily.

"It's called arousal," he responded bluntly.

Alan couldn't control her flush. "Listen, Guy," she said tightly, "I'm confident I can handle the men, thank you very much. Our regulars wouldn't let any new man get out of line. Besides, Dad is sober these days. He's out and about, and Kieran is always around. I have three favourite men in my life. And, no, one of them isn't *you*."

"Lord of the Valley?" he queried, very dryly.

The fact he knew mortified her. "Okay I admit I call you that sometimes."

"You've been calling me that for years," he jeered softly.

"Be that as it may, my three favourite men are Dad, Kieran and Simon—in that order."

He didn't look in the least slighted. In fact he laughed, showing his beautiful even white teeth. "Then, Ms Callaghan, you're in the best of all possible hands."

Inside the house, Alana excused herself quickly. "I won't be more than a few minutes. I'll just wash up. Go into the living room. Make yourself at home."

"Is that one of Kieran's?" Guy made a beeline to the wall hung with a huge, unframed canvas. It was an abstract, yet unmistakably the light-filled Australian bush. It sang of it. It even seemed to smell of it. "Of course it is," Guy muttered to himself. "Couldn't be anyone else's. It's astonishing! It radiates!" He suddenly wanted to buy it, knowing if he suggested such a thing Kieran would have the painting off the wall in no time, gift-wrapped and delivered to him.

"Tell *him* that," Alana called, dashing away.

God knew, Alex had tried often enough to tell him, Guy thought, studying the work of art even more intently. How did Kieran get so much *light* into it? Annabel Callaghan had not painted, to the best of his knowledge, but she had been a very "arty" woman, enormously gifted at craftwork. One of Annabel's Denby cousins was a well-known painter, Marcus Denby, who had lived in England for the past thirty years. So it was in the genes, in their nature, Guy thought. Though it was only since his mother's death that Kieran had found release in these riveting landscapes, "knocked up"—in his own words—in one of the farm sheds. Kieran painted. Alana read books. Alan drank himself to death.

Guy had known Kieran all his life. Kieran was clever, insightful, extremely hard-working but he wasn't meant to be a sheep farmer. It was at Alex's instigation that Guy had discovered Kieran Callaghan's great gift. He simply hadn't known. But Alex *had*. He knew Alex and Kieran, remarkably close in their teens, had long since gone their separate ways. Something hadn't worked out, and he often felt that was a great pity. He had tried at one time to find out what the big rift had been, but both, independently of one another, had let him know he was breaching boundaries. After that he had backed off. Alex had more than her share of admirers anyway. He just hoped she wouldn't settle for poor old Roger. Roger Westcott was a good man—they had gone to school and university together—but he wanted someone with a lot more going for him for his beautiful, artistic sister.

Guy was still standing in front of the painting when Alana flew down the staircase.

"There—what did I tell you? A few minutes!" she announced breathlessly.

He let his eyes rest on her, aware of a powerful desire to reach for her, fold her in his arms, let what might happen, happen. Instead he said lightly, "You look like you've had a shower." She was wearing different clothes—a red tank top and beige shorts that showed off her long beautiful legs. Her honey-blonde hair was damp, little tendrils curling around her hairline like golden petals.

Her face lit up with a smile so beautiful it took his breath. "Just a quick one. In and out. Come through to the kitchen," she invited, almost dancing ahead. "You like that painting of Kieran's, don't you?" she asked over her shoulder. The delicious scent of boronia wafted to him in her wake. Probably the soap she had used. No wonder that new shearer was drooling over her. Was there ever such a bloom on a woman?

"Kieran might be on the wrong track, sticking to wool production," he risked saying. "He has it in him to be a very fine artist. To make it his career."

Alana considered that quietly. "Of course he has," she

agreed, very proud of her brother's outstanding ability. "Do you think I haven't told him that? And I'm sure Alex is tired of telling him. I think they had a big bust-up about it."

"When was this?" He frowned.

She met his eyes. "I have an idea Kieran might have taken to looking in on Alex whenever he's in Sydney. They could have made up, but if they have he's not saying. He goes there a lot at the weekends. He was there recently."

"And he doesn't tell you if he sees her?" Guy's frown deepened.

"Kieran plays his cards very close to his chest when it comes to your beautiful sister," Alana said. "There was a time they were close, but then she moved away, and now Roger Westcott is always in the picture. Alex will never be short of men in love with her. But the specific occasion I'm referring to was last Easter, when we were all in Sydney for the Royal National. They were feinting around one another like a couple of boxers."

"Don't they always?" Guy asked laconically. "Over the years both of them seem to have built up an impenetrable wall. Now, can I help you with anything?"

Alana laughed. "Please sit down. I'm not short, but you *tower* over me."

"Kieran and I are of a height," he pointed out reasonably, pulling out a chair. "Your dad is a big man."

"That's all very well, but you're different somehow. Kieran started painting just after Mum died, when the pain was almost too much to bear. He's very artistic, like Mum. She always used to encourage him with his drawing, from when we were kids. Kieran can draw anything. He's marvellous with trees. A few strokes and he's created a whole hillside of eucalypts."

"Alex is right. He's brilliant."

"Hey, *I'm* right too," she reminded him, pausing in what she was doing. "I know good art when I see it, thank you, Guy."

"Of course you do." His tone soothed. "It's one of the reasons I admire you. You're getting to be a woman for all seasons. All of us are right about Kieran, but Alex is the one in an ideal position to help him."

Alana's expression was sad. "Kieran doesn't *want* to be helped, Guy."

"What does your dad think?"

Alana set out cups, saucers and plates from her mother's best Royal Doulton dinner set. This was Guy Radcliffe, after all. "Dad does his best to understand, but he can't critique Kieran's work. He can't relate to abstract depictions. He doesn't want to see the soul of a tree, or the spirit of the bush. He wants photographic realism. Dad is a bit out of his depth with art. He'd be the first to admit it. What do you want to talk to him about?" She changed the subject to what was really on her mind. "He hasn't borrowed money off you, has he?" She was very fearful he had.

Guy looked back at her directly. "I thought we'd agreed it was a private matter?"

"You know *everything*—we're in a lot of trouble," she said bitterly.

"If your father needs help, I'll give it to him," Guy responded. "Are you going to put the coffee on?"

"You're here to give orders, are you?"

"No, only trying to be helpful."

"Dad has put his whole life into Briar's Ridge," she said, doing just as he suggested. "We were doing just fine until Mum died. Since then, of course, Dad has made a few really bad mistakes."

Guy knew about all of them. "Forgive him for them, Alana. Grief is a terrible thing. The mind doesn't function as well as it should."

"I do forgive him," she said, flashing her beautiful glittery eyes at Guy. "He's my father. I love him. But Kieran and I know we may be forced to sell if we don't do well at the coming sales. The two of us have poured so much hard work into the place—" She broke off to look at him. "I had an idea we could do something like Morgan Creek, in the next valley. What do you think?" She had intended talking to Guy about this at some stage—why not now?

"You mean offer day trips to a working station? Show tourists and visitors the ropes, let them learn about our oldest and biggest industry, give them a great barbecue lunch, let them enjoy whip cracking and boomerang-throwing and then send them on their way?"

"I'm ready to try my hand at it."

"Alana, you're ready to try your hand at *anything*," he said, rather quellingly.

"Like Superwoman?" Her response was sharper than she intended.

"You already work far too hard. Have you given any thought as to how you're going to fund it?" he challenged.

She gave him a look that was hurt and disgusted. "Guy, we have to *fight* to save this place."

He saw behind her aggression to the pain. "Maybe your father has lost the will to fight?" he said gently. "Maybe Kieran would like a crack at another life? And you? What about you, Alana? Are you going to fight to save Briar's Ridge, and then settle down some place else? You'll marry. I'd be surprised if you weren't married by this time next year."

That made Alana grit her teeth. "Are you *nuts?*"

He laughed. "I can't believe someone else hasn't ever suggested it."

She waved that fact away. "If you mention Simon, I tell you, you're on very dangerous ground."

"In that case I'd better back off. I'm fond of my cousin, Alana, but no way is he a match for you. You like bossing everyone around."

It took her half a minute to see he was teasing. "I have to confess to bossing Simon," she said wryly. "But in my own defence I had to do it. If you're so fond of him, why don't you get him away from his mother?"

Guy looked back with his usual calm concentration. "Alana, I *could* get him away from Rebecca—but it would take a miracle to get him away from *you*. Simon has invested everything in you. I don't mean this unkindly, but he's rather like your favourite Border Collie, Monty. He's one-woman loyal. You're Simon's dearest friend, his greatest interest in life—his only love."

She slumped into the chair opposite him, unaware that the oval neck of her tank top had dipped into her lovely young cleavage. "Once upon a time I would never have believed you. Now I think it's scary. Simon *can't* channel all his love into me. Suppose I fall in love with someone? Suppose Dad has to sell the farm and we have to move away? Suppose I die? People get killed all the time. We know that better than most people. He *can't* love me. Besides, his mother wouldn't stand for it. She's drilled it into him that she doesn't even approve of me as a friend. I know she's a relative of sorts, but she's a horrible woman. She's all but broken Simon's spirit."

"Then he ought to hit on some motto—like *Be A Man*. Simon has to develop a little backbone, Alana," he offered crisply, wondering if Simon had ever worked up enough courage to kiss her.

"That's all very well for you to say. Simon is scared of his mother." She hesitated a moment, then soldiered on, "You know Rose quite likes Simon…"

The brackets around his mouth deepened in amusement. "I can see the wheels turning in your golden head. But *you* can't play matchmaker."

"Why don't *you* try your hand at it, then?" she shot back. "You're so highly successful at everything you do."

"Okay!" He leaned back, considering, linking his strong tanned arms behind his crow-black head. "Why don't *I* show a little interest in *you?*" he suggested.

The expression on Alana's face abruptly changed. "What? Pretend a romantic in…ter…est?" She stumbled over the word.

"Why make it sound like there's more chance of getting struck by lightning?" His tone mocked. "Surely it wouldn't be all that difficult? You're a smart girl."

"Men don't like smart girls," she said bluntly.

'Ah, yes, but you're as beautiful as a dream. That helps."

Her eyes looked frightened. "Would you like to walk that by me again? I'm *beautiful?*"

"Would you settle for sexy?"

His gaze tantalised her. "Thanks, but no, thanks, Guy." She whirled up from her chair. "I'll do anything in the world for Simon except fall in love with *you.*"

Kieran was greeted by the incomparable aroma of rich, dark roasted coffee. Alana had made a stack of sandwiches that looked really good, as well as producing a plate of triple chocolate brownies she had made only the night before. Alana was a good cook. Their mother had seen to that. The brownies were a favourite with their father, who nowadays mostly preferred to drink than eat.

Kieran poured himself a cup of coffee, then sat down beside his sister. The pair of them were so golden they delighted the eye. "It's good to see you, Guy." Kieran spoke with warm sincerity. "You don't get over often enough."

"Things will start to slacken off as winter approaches," Guy said. "I was admiring your new landscape in the hallway. It's quite something."

"It's yours!" Kieran declared, strong white teeth biting into a ham sandwich with relish.

It was just as Guy had expected. "I'd be very happy to

own it, Kieran, but I'm speaking to you as a buyer. I'd like to pay for it."

Kieran shook his leonine mane. "That's not going to happen. You've been too good to us, Guy."

"Could you elaborate on that?" Alana looked quickly from one to the other.

"Haven't you noticed all the nice things I do?" Guy told her smoothly. "I've lent you various equipment from time to time. I've sent wine, table grapes, our very best extra virgin olive oil. I've given Kieran here plenty of advice when he's asked."

Kieran spread his arms wide. "You're brilliant, Guy. No wonder Lana's little puppy dog Simon calls you The Man. If you like the painting, Guy, it's yours. I can knock up another one."

But Guy was minded to be serious. "You know you have a considerable gift?"

Kieran's smiling face sobered. "My talent for painting won't keep Briar's Ridge going, Guy. You know that."

"But your talent for painting might carry you far."

"You sound just like Alex." Kieran gulped rather than sipped at his steaming hot coffee. "If Alex had her way I'd be mounting an exhibition before the end of the year. She's guaranteed me a sell-out."

"Alex knows what she's talking about," Guy pointed out, in his quiet, authoritative voice. "She can help you."

Kieran kept silent.

How mysterious were the connections of the heart, Guy thought.

Alana looked across the table, feeling bewildered. "Do you two know something I don't?"

Guy managed a lazy smile. "Lots of things I expect."

Kieran too grinned. The smiles didn't fool her. Alana turned to her brother. "Are we in deeper than you've told me?" she asked, sounding worried.

"We'll know more after the sales, Lana." Kieran picked up another sandwich.

She drew a quick breath. "I've spoken to Guy about my idea of turning Briar's Ridge into a show farm, like Morgan Creek."

Kieran glanced across the wide pine table at Guy, then back at his sister. "Lana, we've been over this. It might work with a big influx of money, but even if by some miracle we could borrow it, Dad wouldn't sit still for it. You know that. He wouldn't want people wandering around the property. He'd hate it."

"So we go under? Is that it?" She blinked furiously, amazed she was so emotional these days.

Kieran laid an arm around his sister's shoulders. "We haven't gone under yet, kiddo!" Brother and sister stayed that way for a moment, then Kieran rose, pocketing a couple of brownies. "That was great. Just what I needed." He looked at Guy with his extraordinarily blue eyes. "Dad's in the Second Paddock, if you want to find him. We're supposed to have a meeting with Bob Turner at three." Bob Turner was the local wool representative. "Want me to drop you out there?"

Guy shook his head. "I won't keep you. I know you've got plenty on your hands. Any of the other locals been around yet?" he asked. The local wool growers usually turned up to check out the quality of their neighbours' clip.

Brother and sister nodded golden heads in unison. "Harry Ainsworth and Jack Humphrey," Kieran said. "The stack's growing, but it's nothing like our best quality. Dad is disappointed, though he really should have been expecting it. I'm keen to see what's happening on Wangaree."

Wangaree's clip always attracted enormous interest. At the important wool sales in Sydney buyers representing the leading woollen mills and the famous fashion houses of the world usually found their clip close to perfection, which meant Guy had a good idea of what Wangaree's clip would bring even before it was auctioned off. No matter the slump in prices, wool of the quality produced by Wangaree could be eagerly snapped up.

"Why don't we make it one day next week?" Guy suggested. "The clip will have grown even taller by then. It's superfine, and unbelievably white. Bring Alana. Stay to lunch. Your father is very welcome too, but I'll speak to him myself when I drive out to see him."

Kieran moved off with the grace of a trained athlete. "That'll be great! By the way, I meant what I said about the painting. It's yours. I refuse to take money for it."

"Then I'll just have to find another way to pay you back," Guy called after him. "I'll have it framed."

"Sure." Kieran waved a hand. "I couldn't run to a frame. Good ones cost the earth."

"After which I'll hang it in a prominent place at the house," Guy promised. "In the years to come I'll be able to say, *Yes, that's a Callaghan. He's a good friend of mine. I was one of the lucky ones. I got in on the ground floor.*"

CHAPTER FOUR

THINGS didn't go well for Briar's Ridge at the sales. Brother and sister sat together at the Wool Exchange in a tense silence as wool worth millions and millions of dollars was sold off. The market was down. No big surprise. Everyone had anticipated that. But mercifully it kicked up quite a bit when the first of the Wangaree Valley clip came up for sale.

"This is awful—the waiting." Alana was so anxious she felt sick to her stomach.

"Listen, it's not that bad." Kieran, nervous himself, but hiding it extremely well, tried to comfort her, even though he had the gut-wrenching feeling it was going to be. This sale represented twelve months' growth of wool and a hell of a lot of hard work from him and Alana. They had virtually carried their father, once such a dynamo.

Wangaree's clip, one of the star attractions of the sale, was recognised as superb. Everyone in the Valley had seen it, marvelling at the quality. Another top producer from the adjoining State of Victoria had called it perfection. Guy's comment had been, "It's better than that. It's *damned good!*" One didn't hear him say that all that often. Guy wasn't one to commit himself, but the Exchange was abuzz with excitement. People in the know were predicting a record price for Wangaree's clip, and as a spin-off maybe others in the Valley.

If she turned her head she would be able to see him, Alana thought. He was sitting with the top people of the industry. In his group would be her uncle Charles—her mother's brother, Charles Denby. Uncle Charles was as good as a stranger to her and Kieran, though their resemblance to their Denby mother was most apparent. In fact, Uncle Charles was so remote he mightn't have been their relative at all. It was no secret he had been deeply shocked when his beautiful sister, Annabel, the apple of everyone's eye, had married a struggling sheep farmer, an Irishman, "rough diamond" Alan Callaghan. And Denby brother and sister had been near enough estranged since the day of the wedding, which unhappily no Denby had attended. A lasting wound.

The three Denby sisters, Violette, Lilli and Rose, dressed to kill and turning heads, fresh from a splendid lunch at one of Sydney's top restaurants, had been present at the inspection earlier, but two had since disappeared—most likely to hit the fashion boutiques. Only Violette remained with her father and—need it be said?—Guy. Violette wouldn't want to miss out on the Denby sales, let alone miss the frenzy of bidding when Wangaree's clip came up.

"I'm glad Dad's not here," Alana sighed, her spirits wilting. Their father had been too nervous to come. Once upon a time he had been right in the thick of it, so proud of having his beautiful wife and family beside him, receiving handshakes and congratulations when his sale prices were good.

An hour later Wangaree's lot came up. It was sold, as predicted, in the blink of an eye, once again to a leading European fashion house. Italian designers had a wonderful way of mixing wool with silk. Alana loved the top designers, their work cut and tailored by people whose ancestors had been handling the finest fabrics for hundreds of years. She remembered how her untrained mother had cut and woven fabric so it fell into the most beautiful soft folds.

By four o'clock the sale was over, with hundreds of lots having gone under the hammer. Alana and Kieran, though heartsore over Briar's Ridge's downspiralling fortunes, remained behind to shake Guy's hand. All eyes were on him as he stood in the centre of the floor, surrounded by prominent people within the industry, head and shoulders above most of them, clearly The Man. Simon had been spot on when he had found this name for his illustrious cousin.

"Don't look now, but Uncle Charles and Vindictive Vi are coming our way," Kieran muttered. "Of course there's the strong possibility they'll spot us and shoot off in the opposite direction."

"And who would care?" Alana asked wearily, fully expecting to be ignored. Charles Denby knew nothing about the milk of human kindness. He was a civilised monster.

"When do you suppose dear old Charles is going to make the transition to a *real* person?" Kieran asked, with a flash of black humour. "I mean, I've never understood a damned thing about the big estrangement. What was so shocking about Mum breaking with family tradition and marrying Dad? The Denbys aren't Royalty, for goodness' sake. Even hell bent on wrecking himself, Dad's still a handsome man. So he was a nobody on the social register? He must have been really something when he was young. Big, handsome, strong. He was hard-working, perfectly respectable. People liked him. He'd even managed to buy himself Briar's Ridge, though it was mortgaged up to the hilt. He didn't take Mum to a hovel. And she loved him. Wasn't that all that mattered?" Kieran broke off angrily, visibly upset.

"One would have thought so!" Alana sighed.

"Oh, no—they haven't spotted us," Keiran groaned in dismay.

Charles and Violette were so busy talking, heads together, probably planning a night out on the town with Guy's party, they all but walked into Alana and Kieran.

"Oh, it's you two!" Violette reacted with her usual hateful disdain. She looked Alana up and down, her gaze deliberately pitying, as though Alana were dressed by charity shops instead of a smart-casual designer.

Alana, well used to her cousin's intended put-downs, took no notice. What consumed her was the look in her brother's eyes. Slow to anger, Kieran had been known to go off like a rocket if sufficiently provoked. It was their father's temper—nearly always under control, but always there. She gave her brother a beseeching look. It would do no good at all for Kieran to lose his temper right here and now.

Ignoring Violette, she addressed her distinguished-looking, ultra-remote uncle. "How are you, Uncle Charles?" she asked politely. "You look well. Congratulations on the Denby prices."

A tall man, Charles Denby stared down at his niece with the strange intensity he always bestowed on her. "Everything we wanted," he announced with ice-cold suavity. "You, on the other hand, mustn't have liked what you heard for the Briar's Ridge lot? I saw it myself. Not up to scratch, my dear. Or rather it'll make up darn scratchy."

Kieran broke in, the heat of anger coming off his powerful, lean body. "Why, sir, do you go out of your way to be so damned cutting?"

Violette's breath exploded in shocked indignation. "I beg your pardon, Kieran?" she huffed. "You apologise to my father this *instant.*"

Kieran gave her a sidelong look that blazed with contempt. "Tell me, *Vi,* you silly, pretentious creature, what is there to apologise for? All our civility, all our polite overtures, get met with freezing dislike. My mother and your father were brother and sister. I could never treat my sister the way your father treated his—no matter what! And my mother did absolutely nothing but marry the man she loved."

Charles Denby's only reaction was a narrowing of his glacial blue eyes. "Your mother brought disgrace on herself and the family," he said finally. "Alan Callaghan was a nothing and a nobody who put my sister in her coffin. Now the whole Valley knows him as a hopeless drunk. Get out of my way, young man. I have better things to do than talk to an upstart like you."

Upstart? The irony was that Kieran looked more like their uncle than he did their own father. Alana sucked in her breath, fully expecting the rocket to launch.

Only Kieran surprised her. He spoke quietly, but his body language was immensely threatening. "There's plenty of room for you to walk around me, sir. Another word and I can't guarantee your safety."

Alarmed, Alana took hold of Kieran's hard-muscled arm—but not before Guy, aware of a mounting crisis, moved swiftly to join them.

"It might be an idea to cool it, Kieran." He came alongside the younger man, keeping his voice low and level. "This *is* the Wool Exchange, and every eye is on us. You're my friend, and I don't want to see you get into trouble."

Kieran shook his leonine head, as if to clear it. "This man here—" he gritted.

"It might be time, Charles, to walk away." Guy glanced meaningfully at Charles Denby.

"That's the trouble with people like you Callaghans," Violette sneered, hot red colour staining her cheekbones. "You simply don't know how to behave. Come on, Daddy, they're not fit to speak to." She spoke as though Alana and Kieran's natural habitat was the gutter.

"Yes, run away!" Kieran told her in a furious undertone, looking as if he was about to give her a good shove. "It's my sister who's the lady around here. Never *you!*"

"Kieran, *please*—if not for our sakes, for Mum's," Alana implored. She was excruciatingly aware a number of people were turning to stare. "Wouldn't she have been horrified to see us make a spectacle of ourselves?"

"Sadistic man!" Kieran rasped, as Charles Denby and his daughter stalked off. He turned his burning blue gaze on Guy. "What have we ever done to them to warrant such treatment?"

Guy's answer was immediate. And it sounded as if it came from the heart. "Your uncle has never been able to face down his demons, Kieran. Charles Denby is a very bitter and unhappy man. It has to be said there was a time he adored his sister, and he continued to do so though he became warped and bitter. What you have to do is let your anger settle. There's nothing you can do to change your uncle. His rigid attitude has deprived him of so much happiness in life. You can't hope to engage his liking or sympathy." He spread his hands. "Charles hasn't anything left to give. He's to be pitied, really."

"I don't pity him," Kieran fumed. "We're sick to death of being ignored and humiliated, Guy, of having our father spoken about with such contempt. How callous can a man get? If he weren't an old fogey I'd have socked him." He stared at his friend, so angry there was a red mist in front of his eyes. "Listen, would Lana be all right with you?" It came out in a plea. "There's someone I must see."

"But of course," Guy answered, as though surprised Kieran would even have to ask.

Alana looked at her brother in consternation. "Who is it? Where are you going?" They hadn't planned anything but a quiet evening, most likely pondering their losses.

"I feel bad, Lana." He looked to her for understanding. "But I need to see someone."

"A woman?" Alana stared at her brother, thinking it quite possible Kieran had a secret life.

"Yes. Of course a woman." He bent to kiss her cheek. "You'll go back to the hotel? I really don't know what time

I'll be in. It could be an hour or hours. But we'll leave as scheduled—first thing after breakfast."

Alana kept her head tilted to him. "What's happening here, Kieran? Who is this mystery woman? She sounds pretty important to you."

"Well, I'm not much use to her," Kieran said with great bitterness. "Look, I have to get out of here."

"Then go," Guy urged him gently. "I'll look after Alana."

"I don't need *anyone* to look after me." Alana turned on Guy, her own temper going up a dozen notches. "Anyway, Guy, you must have plans of your own."

"Which just so happen to include you." He rested his hand briefly on her shoulder. "Off you go, Kieran. Everything's okay here. You, however, look like a man who's in dire need of comfort."

Kieran's blue eyes flashed. 'Thanks, Guy." He transferred his gaze to his sister. "I'll make it up to you, Lana." With that he turned on his heel and stomped away, his tall, powerful body all tightly coiled fury.

They were out on the street, and strong sunlight, even at late afternoon, bounced off the pavement. The sidewalk was busy with people hurrying to and fro; traffic streamed bumper to bumper.

"There's no need for you to bother about me, Guy," Alana said, trying to keep her enormous upset down. Who exactly did her uncle think he was? The next Pope? *"Your mother brought disgrace on herself and the family!"* What did *that* mean? Some words, once uttered, could never be called back. The man was paranoid about family, and insufferably sanctimonious. "I'm perfectly all right on my own."

"I don't think so." He was finely tuned to her mood, and deeply sympathetic.

"You'll want to be with your friends," she persisted doggedly.

"I regard you and Kieran as my friends."

"Gosh, I don't know if we're *fit* to be your friends," she muttered bitterly. "What the hell was my uncle on about? You know everything that goes on in the Valley. I adored my mother. She was a beautiful, dignified, gracious woman. How could she have brought disgrace on herself? Forget her awful family. They're the *real* disgrace. They act like the enemy—except for Rose. How did Rose miss out on their worst characteristics? My mother marrying my father can't possibly explain Uncle Charles's attitude."

"I told you. Charles is a tortured soul. And his wife and daughters have been affected to a greater or lesser degree. Rose, the youngest, is the most fortunate. Most of it has rubbed off on Violette, for which I pity her. Now, why don't we go and grab a cup off coffee?"

"I don't want one," she said mutinously, unaware that the sparkle in her eyes and the colour in her cheeks made her look extraordinarily beautiful.

"Okay—a stiff drink. Don't argue. I want one, even if you don't. You can't do anything about your mother's family, Alana. Don't even try."

"Why do you just pick up and then drop Violette?" she accused him. "You sound on side with her, yet she's so horrible. Could it be you're only interested in her body?"

He glanced down at her rebellious face. "I'll forget you said that, because you're so upset. Here—this will do." He drew her off the pavement into the foyer of one of the city's leading hotels.

"Why don't we check in while we're at it?" she suggested, putting her hand out to catch his arm. "Kieran has a mystery woman. I'm going to get myself a mystery man."

"Well, that lets me out," Guy said evenly." I've known you all your life."

In the handsomely appointed lounge, Alana sank into a comfortable chair. Only a few tables were occupied. Smiles and quiet conversation. It would be another hour before the regulars and the after-work crowd arrived.

"What will it be?" Guy remained standing, his face showing its own brooding tension.

If anything, it only made him look even sexier, she thought, feeling angry, nervy and very, very *physical*. No one brought it out in her like this man.

"Perhaps it's time I took to the whisky?" she said.

"Let's settle for a gin and tonic—or a glass of white wine?"

"It really ought to be champagne. For you, anyway. Congratulations, Guy." She lifted her hazel eyes to him, angry, unshed tears making them diamond-bright. "Kieran and I were waiting behind to tell you that when my awful, *awful*, malevolent relatives walked into us. I have to say it was by mistake. I think they were discussing what was happening tonight."

"It definitely wasn't happening with me," Guy said. "Just try to relax. You've got enough burdens without taking your relatives on board. I'll be back in a minute." He walked away to the bar, with every female eye in the vicinity tracking him. A woman would have to be blind to miss him.

An animal lover, Alana always saw her brother as a golden lion and Guy as a sleek black panther. And where was Kieran going, so completely and utterly furious? It had been blindingly obvious. Of course he had a woman in Sydney. He was a virile young man. Sydney was little over a two hour drive from the Valley. The big hurt was that he hadn't confided in her. She tried to accept that, but the hurt gnawed deep at her. Why hadn't he told her about something so important? He told her just about everything else. Was it possible the mystery woman was married? Oh, that was *so* risky. She would be beautiful, of course. The artist in Kieran would be drawn like a magnet to a beautiful woman. But she couldn't be more beautiful than Alexandra Radcliffe. Alex was really and truly a classic beauty. Although Alex and Kieran operated on different planes.

Guy returned empty handed. "What about my G&T?" she asked in surprise. "Not even a bowl of nuts or a packet of potato chips?" She tried to fight her edginess with banter.

He sat down in the chair nearest her. "There you go again! I've ordered a bottle of champagne."

"Good heavens! Isn't that a dumb thing to do? I'm just so angry and despondent I might get drunk."

"I won't let that happen." He very gently patted her hand, his dark eyes glinting. "You had a good lunch, didn't you?"

"Not as good as yours, I bet." It was usual for the pastoral houses to take the big wool producers to lunch on sales day. "Oh, God, what a day!" she lamented. "We're going to lose Briar's Ridge, Guy. We needed good sales. We're drowning in debt—as if you didn't know."

"Something can be worked out," Guy said.

She looked at him with a sharp sense of humiliation. "You've been propping us up, haven't you? I feel it in my bones."

"You didn't *want* me to try and save you?" He studied her face intently.

She glanced away. Wherever his eyes touched her she felt little jolts of electricity. Even when he took his dark eyes from her, she still felt the after-shocks. "I'd much prefer it if we saved ourselves," she said, in an agony of helplessness, hopelessness—and, it had to be admitted, burning resentment.

"Well, let it go for the moment," Guy advised. "You're right on the edge. So, for that matter, am I."

"*Never!* Not Guy Radcliffe?"

"You don't even know me."

"Yes, well, I know as much as is safe to know. Ah—here comes the champagne."

"Two glasses and I'll take you back to your hotel. I'd like you to have dinner with me tonight."

Her heart almost leapt into her mouth. "You can't be serious? I expect Uncle Charles and Vi will have muscled in?"

"I had the pleasure of Charles and your cousins at lunch."

"If I didn't know better I'd say you found 'the pleasure' quite an ordeal. Has Uncle Charles ever turned the conversation to wedding bells?"

"Nothing so alarming." A waiter, who bore more than a passing resemblance to a well known English comic, arrived with the bottle of champagne, presenting it for Guy's inspection like a character in a skit. After a quick glance, Guy nodded.

"Surely you've sown your wild oats by now?" Alana asked, after the waiter had waltzed his way back through the tables. Was it possible the comedian really was in town and there was a hidden camera?

"Dinner for two," Guy said, watching the waiter's comic progress himself. "Just you and me. I'd much rather listen to you—even if you do like to cross swords." He lifted his glass. Their flutes clinked. "Loosen up, Alana. There are always some compensations available."

She took a quick sip. It was delicious. "Believe me, I want to. But I can't. I'd love to have dinner with you, Guy—not that I've got anything halfway decent to wear—but I suddenly feel I'm wanted at home." She spoke with such urgency she might actually have received a phone call. "Kieran did ring Dad to let him know how things went. Dad's been good for weeks, but I fear he won't be able to handle this. He'll start drinking again." She sought understanding in his eyes. "You couldn't possibly drive me back tonight, could you?" She was so nervous her tongue seemed to be cleaving to the roof of her mouth. "I understand perfectly if you can't. You probably have commitments. Not to mention breakfast with Violette," she added, even though she recognised it was foolish.

"Is this the right way to go about asking me?" He looked steadily back.

"I guess not. But I'm nervous. It's difficult not to be nervous around you."

His mouth compressed. She had a mad urge to lean forward and kiss it, though neither of them were acting in the least flirtatiously.

"I have to say you hide it remarkably well. There's nothing that can't be taken care of at a later date. You really want to go home? You're absolutely sure?"

She took a deep, fluttery breath, then nodded her head. "If you'd be good enough to take me, Guy," she said meekly.

Now he smiled—half-amused, half-mocking. "I rather enjoy seeing you this way, sweet and pleading. But just how do you think you can help your father?"

She stayed quiet, took another sip. "At least I'll *be* there. You know how he is. I can't help worrying. I'll ring Kieran. Let him know. He has his mobile with him. I'm guessing he won't be able to drag himself away from his mystery woman. That's if he finds her. You wouldn't happen to know who she is?"

Guy's eyes were brilliant, but unreadable. "The whole thing is pretty damned weird. But, whoever she is, she clearly has a lot of power over Kieran."

CHAPTER FIVE

SHE wasn't in the apartment when he arrived. Kieran hadn't expected her to be. It would probably be another hour before she got home. He considered ringing her, decided not to. He had his key. He let himself in, instantly inhaling the lovely scent of her. He could almost see her floating towards him. Sometimes he got so frustrated he could punch a hole in the wall.

He turned on a few lights. It was a beautiful apartment. No minimalist approach here. Everywhere one looked there was something beautiful to admire. The colours were white and a delicate shade of green, with accents of sunshine-yellow; there were lots of silk cushions with expensive fringes, tall *famille vert* porcelain vases, valuable antiques someone had turned into lampstands for her. *Lampstands,* mind you. The rich really were different. A glorious cyclamen orchid with five bracts sat in another deep *famille vert* bowl on a glass-topped table.

A beautiful setting for a beautiful woman. He crossed to the sliding glass doors, opened them. Beyond the plant-filled balcony set with a circular table and chairs was Sydney's magnificent harbour, the breeze fresh off it. She had a splendid view, fanning three hundred and sixty degrees. And why not? The apartment had cost millions. Well, they had it. He shrugged. Old money. Nothing ostentatious.

He ripped off his jacket and threw it down over the back of a sofa. He loosened a couple of buttons at the neck of his shirt, jerked his tie down. Next he moved to the cabinet where he knew the drinks were housed. God, how he needed one! He almost began to see how their father had made the tragic slide into alcoholism. Yet hadn't love been the cause of it? The intensity of that love? Surely there was something a little noble about that? He hadn't just lost his money or his farm. He'd lost a woman—his beloved wife. Their father was grieving so profoundly over the loss of their mother he couldn't seem to face life without her. How would it feel to love someone like that and know you could never have them, let alone have them *back?* Kieran thought he knew.

Whisky came to hand. Great! He poured himself a good shot of it, then walked through to the bright and open kitchen for a little crushed ice from the refrigerator door. This was one neat woman. Not a thing out of place, and lovely little feminine touches everywhere. She loved flowers. He had never seen the apartment without flowers in every room, and that included the en suite and the guest bathroom. Today there were yellow tulips on the glossy black granite flecked with gold. There were lots of crisp white cupboards, some glass-paned to show off fancy bone china, but the *pièce de resistance* of this beautiful apartment, with all its art works and *objets d'art* was always *her.*

Gradually, under such a benign influence, he was calming. What a terrible day! No way could they afford to hold on to Briar's Ridge now. The bank would foreclose on them. And what then? He had come to realise the farm wasn't everything in life to him, as it was to their father and Alana. Alana was a true country girl. She revelled in life on the land. He had always enjoyed it too, but in his heart of hearts he knew he wouldn't mourn the loss of it deeply. He could always visit it when he wanted. He could always paint it when the urge took him.

The truth was, he recognised inside himself that he had a gift. His mother had always told him he did.

"Why, I do believe, my darling Kieran, one day you'll have it in you to become a fine painter. I'd be interested to see what Marcus thinks of all these drawings. Next time he's in the country I'll ask him."

He might never rise to Marcus Denby's lofty heights, but then he had a *different* vision. He wouldn't mind struggling for a while. Just about everyone had to struggle for a while. His abrupt laugh sounded strangely harsh in the silence of the lovely room. He wouldn't have to struggle with Alex by his side. Alex was a Radcliffe, an heiress, a glittering, impossible prize. He threw back the whisky with one gulp. A vision of Alex flashed before his eyes. Skin like a pearl. Eyes and hair like ebony. The pure face of a Madonna, yet she had sinned deeply. He walked to one of the upholstered custom-built sofas and eased his long body into it, staring sightlessly at the exquisite spray of cyclamen orchids. He felt his heart contract with his own kind of grief. That whisky had gone down too quickly. He'd have another…

Immediately he heard the key inserted into the deadlock he jumped to his feet. His heart was thudding, picking up knots. It was dark now. He had turned the lights on. How many times had he entered her apartment before she'd arrived home? He couldn't begin to count.

She must have realised he was there, because she called softly, "Kieran?"

He covered the distance that separated them in a couple of long strides, watching her drop her leather handbag to the silk rug. He reached for her, pulling her into his arms, kissing her feverishly, hotly, hungrily, forcing open her softly cushioned lips.

"I'm crazy about you!" he muttered "Crazy. Is it ever going to stop?" He didn't seem to care that he was overwhelming her with his intensity.

He had her moaning in his arms. To hear her moan meant everything to him. Somehow he had lifted her clear of the ground, crushing her in his powerful grip. She was tall, but so slender, she was a featherweight to him. Her beautiful pale pink suit had little covered buttons down the front. She wore a white silk camisole beneath the jacket. His hand swept rapaciously across her breasts as though it had a life of its own. "Alex, Alex," he whispered. "What am I going to do about you?"

She breathed into his neck. "Just keep on putting me through hell?"

His response was to swing her off her feet, carrying her down the passageway into the master bedroom. He was desperate to be inside her. He couldn't see straight until he was. He threw her down on her marvellous big bed, pausing for a moment to stare down at her as she lay back against the opulent cream and gold quilt. Oh, the *ache* in him! Every time he laid eyes on her he had the sensation that his heart was breaking. Her wonderful dark eyes were huge with emotion. He never felt guilty at seeing her drowning in it. *She* was the one who should feel guilty but refused to. Her arms were thrown back above her head, outstretched, imploring, pleading. She was imperceptibly trembling. Her long silky hair that had been arranged in some elegant knot was coming loose. A skein fell like a black satin ribbon across her pearly cheek.

"How beautiful you are," he rasped. "*Too* beautiful!" But she could never wipe the slate clean.

He reached down to her, his long fingers beginning to burrow at all those little buttons. She made no effort to stop him. She lay quietly while he undressed her, wondering if there was ever going to be an end to this unquenchable desire.

"Why didn't you let me know you were coming?" she whispered.

He made no reply. Instead he pulled her up so he could release the catch on her rose lace bra and expose her exquisite white breasts. How incredibly seductive a woman's breasts were. Every time he undressed her it was like the first time. Such beauty! Always for *him*.

"Kieran—Kieran, do you love me?" Tears filled her large oval eyes.

He kissed them. "How can I love you after what you did to us?" he answered jaggedly. "I *want* you. I *need* you. Be content with that."

They had everything and nothing. All the world lost. "How easily you've condemned me all these years. You had no difficulty at all, even when I told you the truth."

He choked off a bitter laugh. "*Don't,* Alex," he said. "I'm supremely indifferent to your lies. They've all been done to death anyway."

A glistening tear slid down her cheek. She arched her back to make it easier for him to take off her panties—rose lace to match her delicate bra. She always wore the most beautiful underwear. He thrilled to strip the delicate garments off her.

Finally she was naked, her white body as remarkably virginal as when he had first seen it when they were innocent teenagers. There had been no adolescent yearning, no clumsy gropings. It had been full on, wildly passionate sex—she surrendering herself completely, he taking her, penetrating her, as if he wanted his whole self to disappear inside her. Neither of them had been able to get enough of the other. Drunk on sex. Drunk on love. Alex had been his sun, moon and stars.

But almost seven years had passed. Years spent apart. Time they could no longer spend together. He wanted her more now than he had then—barely believable but utterly true. Not only that, he knew how to get more of her. Oh, yes, he did. Alex was *his*. His incurable addiction.

He fell to his knees beside the bed, still fully clothed,

taking a coral pink nipple sweet as a fruit into his mouth, lightly between his teeth… "Alex, Alex, Alex…" he whispered, his voice fierce even to his own ears.

She shaped his golden head with her hands, sinking her fingers into his thick mane of hair. Her eyes were filled not only with an overwhelming desire, but with a deep, dark tenderness. She would have died for Kieran. He knew that. But he didn't care.

He put one strong hand beneath her back, raising her to him.

"Why do I let you do this to me?" she gasped.

He pressed his open mouth all over her. "You know why," he muttered, without a shred of sympathy. "Because neither of us can *stop*."

The big car ate up the miles. Alana thought she might close her eyes briefly, but was stunned when she heard Guy's voice murmur near her ear. "Wake up, Sleeping Beauty."

She blinked and sat straight, looking around dazedly. "I can't believe that! I fell asleep."

"I'd say you needed it." He didn't mention she had been making little distressed whimpers that smote his heart.

"We're home!"

"Right at your door, my lady!" Guy looked very soberly towards the darkened homestead. There appeared to be only one light on, towards the rear of the house. "I'll come in with you." He released his seat belt.

Voices said such a lot about a person, Alana thought. Who you were. What you were. Where you lived, even how you lived. Were you confident, self-assured, charming? Warm or cold, diffident, abrasive, a person to steer clear of. Her father was right. Guy Radcliffe was a *prince*.

They were walking towards the front steps when Buddy, stick-thin no matter how much he ate, emerged from the interior of the house and moved out onto the verandah. He lifted a hand to turn on the verandah light, splashing himself in a dull golden light.

"Miss Lana, I didn't know you'd be comin' home," he called, then tiptoed over to the timber balustrade. "Good evening, Mr Radcliffe," he added respectfully.

"Evening, Buddy." Guy's tone was warm and approving. He knew that approval gave the loyal youngster pleasure and confidence. "Everything okay here?"

They all knew it was nothing of the sort. Alana ran on ahead, up the steps, disappearing into the house.

Buddy's liquid black eyes cut to Guy. "Mr Alan—he start drinkin' a few hours back," he confided in an unhappy voice. "I came to check on 'im. He likes me around."

"I know he does, Buddy." Guy nodded, feeling the keenest sympathy for Alana. "You're a good man to have around."

"I do me best." Buddy glowed at Guy's praise. "I'm afraid Miss Lana is going to find her dad collapsed in his armchair. I wanted to shift him into bed, but he's a big man." He spread his arms an unbelievable distance, to demonstrate just how big. "Didn't have a chance of lifting 'im. It's all so sad."

It's that! Guy thought to himself. What had happened to Alan Callaghan came under the category of "survivor's guilt." Callaghan blamed himself terribly for surviving when the wife he adored hadn't.

"Mrs Annabel, she's up there." Buddy pointed towards the glittering river of diamonds that was the Milky Way. "She's fine. She's not alone. Mr Alan should find somethin' good."

Guy couldn't help but agree. It would allow the man some release. "You can go along now, Buddy," he said. "And thank you. I should be able to get Mr Callaghan into bed."

"Need a hand?" Buddy, thin as a whippet, even in riding boots only five-five, was desperate to help in any way he could.

"Thanks, Buddy, but I'll manage." Guy made a movement to go inside, paused. "Have you eaten yet?"

"No, sir. Been here." Buddy's coal-black curls bobbed as he shook his head. "I had to attend to Mr Alan first."

"Do this for me?" Guy said, as though asking a favour. "Drive out to the estate restaurant and get yourself a really nice meal? Whatever you want—three courses. You can take it away if you feel shy being on your own. I'll ring ahead so they'll know you're coming."

Buddy gave a funny little whoop. "Me?"

"Yes, Buddy," Guy confirmed. "You must be starving by now."

"I am a bit hungry," Buddy admitted. Actually, he had a growling stomach. But the Radcliffe Estate restaurant! He'd only poked his head in a couple of times. Never been in there, of course. It was way too grand for the likes of him. Could he really order up a three course meal? Maybe oysters and a fillet steak? Some crazy wicked chocolate dessert? Mr Radcliffe said he could, and Mr Radcliffe owned the place. Cool!

Alana knelt beside her father's armchair. Alan Callaghan sat in it, looking hellish, one large brown hand resting on the top of her shining head.

"Guy!' Recognition leapt into the bleary red-rimmed eyes as Guy approached. "God, I'm sorry." Her father's normally attractive voice was nothing more than a slurred croak.

"Why don't we get you to bed, Alan?" Guy said, calm as a stone Buddha on the outside, deeply perturbed on the inside. He stripped off his checked jacket.

"Sall right!" Alan Callaghan made a pathetic attempt to heave himself out of the armchair and fell back, looking worse than ever.

"Come on—we'll help you, Dad." Alana fiercely wiped a tear from her cheek with the back of her hand.

"It's okay, Alana. Just get out of the way," Guy told her, in a kindly but authoritative tone.

She didn't argue. Guy said he could do it. Simple. She did what she was told, running ahead to make sure her father's bed was ready and the room was fit to be seen. She was agonisingly embarrassed, but at least she always did her best to make sure her father's bolt hole—for that was what it was—was clean.

They came slowly down the hallway, Guy supporting her father by the shoulders as though Alan Callaghan were a drunken dancing partner. Both dark heads were bent towards their feet. Her father was muttering incoherently to himself. Guy wasn't even breathing hard. It only took a few minutes for Guy to lower the older man onto the narrow bed.

"What is he doing in *here?*" Guy looked about him. "It's a monk's cell."

"With Dad the penitent?" Strain and mortification were showing on Alana's face. "I'm only surprised he doesn't scourge himself."

"I'll undress him," Guy said. "Or at least make him more comfortable. No problem. Go along now."

Alana turned, but hesitated near the door. Her father blew out a harsh, spluttering moan, then seemed to come alive. He lifted one still powerful arm and began to wave it with a vigour that surprised her.

"She was in love with him, you know," he said, in voice that was almost normal. "I'm telling the truth here. I made her pregnant. I made my beautiful Belle pregnant. Can't say anything in my own defence. I did it. I *did it.*" Alan Callaghan made a futile grab for the front of Guy's shirt. "You're a gentleman, aren't yah? And your dad was a gentleman. I'm just a bog Irishman. Anything to say?"

Guy's expression transfixed Alana. It had turned from compassionate to granite. Would this man who had always been so kind to her father now turn and condemn him for being a pitiful drunk? "You're shocking your daughter, Alan," Guy said quietly.

Alan Callaghan stared blearily past Guy, the full weight of

what he had just said seeming to fall on him. "Are yah still here, darlin'?" he asked in dismay.

Alana didn't answer. She stood frozen on the spot, more vulnerable than she had ever been in her life.

"Leave this to me, Alana," Guy repeated, putting his tall rangy body between her and her father.

"What?" She stared at him dazedly. "You *know* what Dad's saying. You *know*—don't you, Guy. And my uncle knows. That's why he hates us."

"Doesn't he just?" Alan Callaghan suddenly bellowed. "He's never tried to conceal it. Idolised her, he did, his beautiful sister. Loved his dear friend David. But I didn't care how I got her. I was mad for her. Just couldn't back off. I always had a touch of the prize fighter in me."

"You're not putting up any fight now, Alan." Guy's dark eyes were blazing with light. "I see no sign of the fighter. Look at you. A big man—what? Fifty-five, fifty-six years of age?— collapsed in your bed like you've been defeated."

Alana was seized by agitation. "Dad's no coward, Guy!" she cried. "He has courage." Or once he had had it, she thought mournfully. But now her father had lost all direction.

Guy bent his gaze on her. "Someone once said courage in a man is enduring in silence whatever heaven sends him."

"What about what heaven takes away?" she retorted fierily. "Takes away so you can never get it back?"

Guy sighed deeply. "We all bear the weight of our losses, Alana. I miss my father every day. He was a fine upstanding man. The *finest*."

At that, Alan Callaghan's broken laugh exploded. "That he was!" he roared, and then, as though all played out he rolled away without another sound. Face to the wall.

It was the worst of all possible scenarios. Alana sat rigid, arms clasped around her, in the living room, waiting for

Guy to come out of her father's room—the cell of the condemned man.

What had her father done all those years ago? What tricks had he used to get the woman he had always looked at so adoringly? How had her mother agreed to marry him, have his baby, when she'd been meant for somebody else? Had *loved* somebody else? Or was there little truth in that either? What else could she hope to find out when her father was drunk?

Guy had known what had been hidden from her and Kieran all along. He had never breathed a word. Surely other people in the Valley knew of the old love triangle? Why had everyone, including her uncle, kept the old story so deeply hidden? And the stark way Guy had spoken! Should he have rubbed in her father's defeat? Could she forgive or forget that? The real nightmare was that Guy himself might hate them underneath. How would she know? What really lay in the depths of his unfathomable dark eyes? And what of Guy's mother, always civil, but maintaining her distance? Guy loved his mother. Sidonie would have known about an old love affair of her husband's, surely? It hadn't gone as far as an engagement, but it now appeared to have been serious. Maybe her mother and David Radcliffe had never patched up a violent quarrel? It happened. Maybe they had argued about the Irishman Alan Callaghan? Was the truth more shocking yet? Whatever it was, it haunted her father—maybe to the grave. It was his choice to walk a self-destructive path.

"He's dead to the world," Guy announced when he returned.

It couldn't have sounded more grim. "Who? The coward?" she retorted, feeling the stinging heat of humiliation.

"I didn't use that word, Alana," he said almost wearily. "You did. But isn't he, in a fashion?" Guy's tone was extraordinarily bitter for him.

He sank onto the leather sofa opposite her, the teak chest that served as a coffee table between them.

"And I thought you were a compassionate man." She stared at him with deeply wounded eyes.

"Compassion isn't working, Alana," he responded bluntly, finally convinced of the fact. "Your father has taken a tremendous blow in life, losing his beloved spouse. But so have others in the Valley—including my own mother. The world is full of people who have had massive blows to overcome. Your father calls himself a fighter? Well, as a fighter, he has hit the mat. Anyone can forgive him that. But he's never tried to get up, Alana. That's the thing. He has you and Kieran. He has Briar's Ridge. He's as good as lost it."

Her voice shook with emotion. "You think I don't *know* that?"

He leaned forward, focusing on her distressed face with its large expressive eyes. "You've put your heart and soul into the farm, Alana. Don't you deserve some consideration? And Kieran has worked like a slave. Though Kieran will fall on his feet. Kieran has inherited the Denby gift."

"No sign of any gift in *me?*" She flashed him a look that was more poignant than bitter. Did he despise her?

"Alana, you're beautiful, and gifted in so many ways," he said with a curious sadness. "What I hate is that so much weight has been put on your shoulders. You should be enjoying a better life, not spending your time fighting off ruin."

The humiliation of it all rendered her abruptly furious. "I *love* my life, Guy!" she said, leaping to her feet. "The last thing I need from you is *pity!* I *hate* it! And never, *never* from you!" Easier that the entire world should pity her.

His response came fast. In a single explosive movement he was on her side of the table, towering over her, his own disturbed emotions in full view. "That's how you see it? *Pity?*"

She stared up at him with a thudding heart, knowing that a challenging answer would change everything in one indelible second. Still she threw out the challenge. "What *else* is it?" She lifted her chin, trying to hold her nerve, yet knowing she was in some kind of jeopardy.

Black eyes that smouldered caught fire. "Well, here's where we find out!"

She couldn't look away The intensity of his expression chopped off her breath. She had set herself against him for years now, but he was about to prove who was in control.

He hauled her to him so her head snapped back, then seemed to fall in slow motion into the crook of his arm. Her hair spilled everywhere in a wild golden mass.

She had the disorienting sensation she was falling… falling…toppling from a very high place with no way to stop. Or would he save her? But this was a wholly different Guy. One she had barely glimpsed. She was confronted by the dominant male pushed that little bit too far. The hunter in him was about to take what he wanted. She couldn't get her breath for the overwhelming excitement.

"Guy—please don't!" It would be the end of their relationship as she had known it.

"Stop me if you can!"

Pulses of electricity were running up and down her thighs, pooling in the delta of her body, alive with raw nerve-endings.

"Guy!" Her voice shook with panic. She felt the *force* of him, the inner energy, the demands he was going to make on her. Everything about him gave her to understand beyond any possible doubt that he desired her above anything else.

Her heart beat as if wings were unfurling in her chest. It was as though she had never been up close to a man in her life, had never known the violent eroticism of a man's hard body, so powerful, so aggressive, so very different from her own.

He was deaf to her involuntary cry—if he even heard her. This was all about getting what *he* wanted. His mouth, poised over hers, abruptly came down, opening her lips beneath his, pressing without crushing, gaining control and then mastery. She had no defence against him. Not even the desire to protect herself. What was happening was *ravishing,* far from gentle, and deeper than hunger. What could it be? The only possible answer was *passion.* She had no recourse but to yield to it— because in the end wasn't this what she craved? All she could do was cling to him, trapped by a sexual pleasure that was nigh on unbearable.

The scent of him was in her nostrils. She felt the indescribable warmth of his mouth and his mating tongue, the taste, the texture, the faint rasp from his tanned polished skin on her tender flesh. She thought dazedly that their mouths were refusing to part. Refusing to surrender the fabulous thrill. Her back arched at the same time as she let out a whimper. What she feared that was she would lose all coherent thought.

His voice, strangely laboured, came from above her head. "Not much pity there, Alana," he said, with unfamiliar harshness.

She thought if he took his encompassing arms away she would simply fold. "No…" She couldn't deny it. There were tears in her eyes. "What *was* your intention?" she whispered. "To teach me a lesson?"

His spread fingers pressed along her spine. "I don't want to discuss it."

"You're so very good at it. Would you like to feel my heart?"

She hadn't believed for one moment that he would respond to what was no more than a taunt. Instead he confounded her. He pushed his hand inside the printed silk of her shirt, the palm of his hand taking the weight of her breast, thinly covered by her bra.

She gasped, instantly suffused in heat. His fingers, manlike, sought her naked flesh. She gripped his wrist tight. She had to stop him, even though she desperately wanted him to keep going. It filled her up with a reckless passion she had never experienced before. Where was her life going? She thought wildly. She had never thought of him as a lover.

Liar, said that inexorable voice inside her.

"Your heart's racing," he murmured, continuing to caress her. His expression was drawn taut, intent, as if he had started on a long-awaited voyage of discovery of her body.

Speech was impossible. Indeed, how could they ever speak to each other after *this?* The tips of his fingers had found her sensitised nipple, full of colour, were rolling it between them so it became a swollen bud of pure want. With one arm he brought her closer into him, staring down into her flushed face.

"You're a beautiful, beautiful woman, Alana!"

"One you shouldn't be putting at risk."

"Close your eyes. I won't hurt you," he promised. "I only want to make love to you a little."

Couldn't he see her agitation? Her flesh was threatening to catch fire. "And if I say you can't?"

"I know I can." His kisses moved to her throat. "Your father will sleep well into the morning. I want to take you home with me." His voice was so low and seductive it could have melted stone.

She knew if she went with him it would be momentous turning point in her life. "Don't think I'm so foolish." Caution welled. She *was* a virgin. She had no protection.

"I won't do anything you don't want. Instinct tells me you're a virgin?" He came at it directly.

A groan escaped her. "What am I, anyway? An open book?" She tried to pull away, but he held her tighter.

"A book I desperately want to read," he said, the note in his voice making her senses swim. "I'll call the house. You've had nothing to eat. I'll get Gwen to make us something."

"And for the rest of the night?" She threw back her golden head, the spirit of challenge showing in her eyes.

'I'll make love to you a little," he said softly. "Though the time's fast approaching to make it real."

"It's real enough for me now," she said, feeling her every last defence had been shaken loose. "Besides, I'm not in such a hurry. I should stay here—where I belong." Her feelings were so intense, so out of control, she felt she had little option but to push the panic button.

"You're too frightened to come with me?" He looked deeply into her eyes.

Insane as it was, it was true. "I have to think ahead, Guy," she answered, grappling with her heart's desire. "If I go to Wangaree with you, the whole Valley will know by the morning."

"Don't be ridiculous," he said. "My people will see you for exactly what you are. A lifelong friend."

"Of course—you *would* command absolute loyalty. Is that how I've never heard even a whisper about my mother and your father? Were they lovers?" She stepped closer, staring into his eyes.

"What would be the point of discussing it?" he said sombrely.

"Point being some people are feeling the shock waves to this day. How did your mother manage to live her life with such a secret in the background?"

He didn't answer for a moment, his striking face taking on a daunting expression. "Why don't we leave my mother out of this, Alana?"

"I'm sorry," she apologised. "But can't you see I have a need, indeed a *right* to know? I'm not a child. I can't be kept in the dark. You wouldn't accept being shut out for a half a minute. Why should I? Your mother must have known. For that matter, when did *you* first find out? Does Alex know? Or was she kept in the dark like me?"

"Keep probing and you'll finish up in a dark forest," he warned, reaching for his jacket. "For the last time—are you coming?"

She braced herself against the intolerable weight of longing. She knew she couldn't resist him. And, to make her position even more vulnerable, she knew of the powerful forces that had gathered in him.

"No, Guy," she said, as though she had sworn an oath. She turned away with a little broken laugh. "I can't think *any* woman has said no to you before."

"Is that why you're doing it?" he asked, his black eyes glittering.

She struggled to frame the right words. "You know why I'm doing it, Guy. You say you don't want to hurt me, but I fear somewhere deep down inside of you, you *do!*"

CHAPTER SIX

KIERAN returned from Sydney, strained and on edge. Although he apologised to Alana for having disappeared on the day of the sales, the name of his mystery woman remained a secret.

So many secrets, Alana thought, herself so troubled in her mind that she left her brother well alone. Kieran would confide in her when he was ready, she reasoned. Until then she would keep out of his private affairs. They only appeared to hold anger and pain. Besides, hadn't her own life turned into a mess?

Like Kieran, she couldn't bring herself to discuss it. She couldn't imagine what Kieran would think if she suddenly confided she was totally in love with Guy Radcliffe. She thought after the initial shock he would advise her to leave well alone. That was the way it must have been with him and Alex. *Leave well alone.* Clearly Kieran believed the Radcliffes were out of reach. The Radcliffes were rich folk. The Callaghans were battlers.

Their father had fought his way out of his binge, but he had lost so much weight for a man previously so strongly built that Alana began to worry his alcohol addiction over the past three years had done significant damage to his body—in particular, his liver. She began to read up all she could about the chronic liver disease cirrhosis, and found her way to an important medicinal herb, St Mary's Thistle, which had been used to good effect for liver ailments, indeed all sorts of ailments, since the time of the ancient Greeks and Romans. Her father refused point-blank to see a doctor and undergo any tests, but he did consent to swallowing the liquid extract the long-established village pharmacist recommended.

"Your dad really needs to see one of the doctors at the clinic, Alana." Kindly eyes were fixed on her. "Don Cameron is a good man. This Milk Thistle here could be no help at all."

Alana thought it was worth a try.

Out of the blue her cousin Rose rang to invite her to lunch at the hugely popular Radcliffe Estate Restaurant.

"I have some news for you!" Rose trilled excitedly down the phone. "I'm up in the air about it, actually. See you Tuesday—say about one p.m.? My shout. I'll make the reservation. It's usually packed out."

Tuesday morning, Alana dressed with care in a brilliantly white linen shirt with a small stand-up collar, over narrowly cut black pants. She had just the legs for the cut, and the right kind of derrière. Around her waist she slung a wide patent leather black belt with a big silver buckle, and she slipped on a pair of high heeled black sandals—her best. Her mother's black bag was dateless, never out of fashion. She thought she looked pretty good. She had inherited her mother's chic, and that actually meant a lot. Money wasn't synonymous with style.

She was looking forward to seeing Rose. All dressed, she presented herself to her father, who was sitting aimlessly in a planter's chair out on the verandah, staring up at the blue hills.

"How do I look?" She struck a model's pose, trying to get a smile out of him. Off the wagon, Alan Callaghan was more morose than on it.

"Beautiful!" he said, putting his arm out to her and gathering her in around her slender hips. "Remember me to little Rosie. Some people just suit their names."

Alana remained in her father's embrace. "Like some people look exactly what they are." Of course she was thinking of Guy—The Man. "What are you going to do with yourself, Dad?"

He grimaced. "Well, let's see. Where shall I start? I thought I might go into town."

"Really?" Alana was pleasantly surprised. Her father rarely wanted to go anywhere. "Why didn't you say? I could have run you in and picked you up later."

"Only just thought of it," he said. "Might call in on Father Brennan. Make me confession."

"Dad?" Alana bent to stare into her father's face, feeling a shock of alarm.

"Only jokin', darlin'." He raised the ghost of a grin. "I haven't been to confession for many years. Hardly time to be starting up again now. But I like Terry Brennan. He's a good bloke."

"Mum thought so." Her mother had been raised a Catholic.

"God bless her!" Alan Callaghan sighed. "She was a saint to put up with me."

"You weren't so bad!" Alana shook him lightly. In fact in the old days their father had been full of fun and good cheer— the most affectionate of fathers. "Mum loved you."

"Did she?"

That struck a badly discordant note. "What are you saying, Dad? Of course she did."

"There's love and there's *love*," Callaghan pronounced flatly.

"So what are you trying to tell me?" Alana asked in distress. Oh, God!

"I let a *dream* rule my life, me darlin'. The dream that your mother loved me. I know she settled for me. I know she was absolutely loyal to me. But I wasn't what she wanted."

Pain slashed all the way through her. "Who *was?* I'm

really confused about all this, Dad. We were a happy family. It wasn't a dream. It was a reality. And Mum *did* love you. She *had* to. She laughed at all your jokes. Don't shatter what we had with maudlin thoughts. Maybe she was in love with David Radcliffe at some stage, when they were very young. But she didn't marry him, did she? She married you."

Alan Callaghan let out a strangled sigh. "Things happen, Alana."

"*Tell* me." She waited, breathless. "It's obviously eating away at you, whatever it is."

"Sorry, darlin'!" Her father sat up straight. "I'm a bit hazy on it myself. You go off now and enjoy yourself. God knows, you deserve a bit of pleasure."

Alana glanced at her watch. She *had* to go, or she would be running late. She had intended taking the car—the air-conditioning in the ute was on the blink—but now she changed her mind. "I'll take the ute. You take the car," she suggested, in her usual generous fashion. Her father didn't know the air-conditioning in the ute was shot. There was so much he didn't know or care about.

"Doesn't matter to me, darlin'," Alan Callaghan said. 'You're all dressed up. *You* take it."

"The car will suit you better," she replied. Alan Callaghan was six-three, like his son, and his skin had a peculiar flush. "I'm fine in the ute." She bent to kiss his cheek, resting one hand on his shoulder. "You have clean shirts in your wardrobe, all ironed. Blue always looks so nice on you. Take care now, Dad. Love you."

"Love you too, my darlin'," Alan Callaghan said, rising his feet, then going to the verandah balustrade to wave her off.

Alana saw pleasure leap into Rose's eyes as she walked towards her. Rose was already seated at the table, having arrived some minutes earlier. She jumped up to hug and kiss her cousin.

"Oh, isn't this great? I'm so happy to see you, Lana," she said in her affectionate way. "You look *gorgeous*—as usual. *Très chic!* You're easily the most stunning girl in the Valley. It puts Vi's nose out of joint I can tell you." She giggled.

"Is it any wonder I love you so much?" Alana asked indulgently. Rose herself looked a picture, in a designer dress that must have cost the earth. Her Italian handbag alone would have set her trust fund back a few thousand dollars. With maybe another thousand or more tied up in the shoes. The Denby girls weren't cheap dressers. They were fashion icons. In fact Alana rarely saw them in the same thing twice.

Predictably, they had been allotted one of the restaurant's best tables, beside the huge floor-to-ceiling plate glass windows. The building was shaded by extensive covered verandahs that commanded a splendid view over the sun drenched vale of vines that marched in precise lines right up to the base of the green foothills. What a visual delight! Alana felt herself calming. It was marvellous paintable country! The ripened chardonnay grapes were to be harvested at any moment, which accounted for the palpable air of expectancy that permeated the air, and it was a sparkling scene laid out for their delectation beneath a shimmering blue sky.

"You're going to have a glass of wine, aren't you?" Rose asked, fixing her cousin with her huge, heavily lashed blue eyes.

Rose was so very, very pretty, Alana thought. Rather like the pin-up girls of old, with her thick blonde hair cut in a bob and her rosebud mouth painted fire-engine-red. And she was sweet. She'd be perfect for Simon. Even the Draconian Rebecca couldn't object that much to Rose Denby.

"Just the one, Rose," Alana said with a smile. "I'm driving."

"Simon is going to run me home," Rose confided, looking just the faintest bit anxious, as if Alana might have some objection. "We'll soon be working together." She held up a hand. "You can't tell him yet, it's not set in stone, but Guy has offered me a job."

"That's your news?" Alana wondered at the reason behind Guy's sudden action.

"Yes!" Rose came across as thrilled. "I think it's right down my alley, but I wanted to get your take on it. You're the one with the good head on your shoulders. I'm a twit."

"That's not right, Rose," Alana protested right away. Pretty as she was, Rose didn't have a lot of self-esteem. "When did you stop believing in yourself? You were an excellent student."

"Sure!" Rose sighed, looking away, across the luxuriant vineyard. "It's hard to believe in yourself with sisters like mine. They gang up on me, those two. I know I was good at school but I've never amounted to anything, have I? You've been working your butt off since Aunt Belle died. People speak of you with such admiration. They dismiss *me* with a little knowing nod—*airhead, featherbrain, fluttery little playgirl.*"

"Hey, that's not true!" Alana caught her cousin's hand and shook it. "You're so hard on yourself, Rose. You're not reaching out, that's all. You can *do* things. You don't have to party all the time. I think it's great Guy has offered you a job. I'm so happy for you."

"You always did have a lot more faith in me than anyone else." Rose leaned across the table, speaking in such a confidential voice that all the people in the huge room might have been dead set on eavesdropping. "I'll be the PR person. I wouldn't be waiting tables or anything like that. Mummy and Daddy would have a fit. It's the social scene I'm good at, but I suddenly realise I *want* a job. I think it's a dumb mistake, the way I've been living the life of a playgirl. Just like you said, I want to *do* something. Not something terribly serious, or really hard work, like you, but something I can enjoy. Something I can shine at. I'm good with people. Unlike my snooty sisters, people seem to like me."

"Well, there's a very good reason for that, Rose," Alana said. "You have charm. You're lovely to look at. You're warm, friendly, intelligent. If you knew anything about mustering sheep I'd hire you myself. But you know everything about the Valley. And you've been just about everywhere in the world, so you can relate to all the overseas tourists. I think you'd be great! Congratulations. I'm proud of you."

Guy's hand is behind everything, Alana thought.

Rose blushed. "Gosh, it makes me happy to hear you say that, Lana. Guy has faith in me too. That means such a lot. I won't let you down. I'll be organising tours of the estate, making sure everything is working smoothly. I expect my duties will grow—Guy said it's up to me. And I can help Simon in the office when I have the time. I've always had a soft spot for Simon, but he can't see *anyone* outside you," she lamented.

Alana shook her head. "Rose, it's high time I told you I have *no* romantic interest in Simon. None whatsoever. We're pals."

Rose blinked, clearly having difficulty accepting what Alana had just said. "But Vi has been telling everyone you two are just biding your time before you get married. Simon's mother is a bit of a pain in the neck, no?" Rose looked at Alana sympathetically. Rebecca Radcliffe, The Widow, had terrified her as a child. Rebecca looked just like the wicked stepmother in her illustrated book of *Snow White*.

"You're not listening, Rosie." Alana placed her hand over her cousin's, giving it several little emphasising taps. "I-am-not-and-never-will-be-in-love-with-Simon."

"Oh, thank you—thank you!" Rose put a hand to her breast, as if she was about to have a heart attack. "Just when I thought you were two steps away from the altar."

"I'm two steps away from punching Vi in the nose," Alana said as though ready to do it.

"But he worships you…" Rose could barely take in this new development.

"He would worship *you* if you played your cards right." Alana looked her cousin directly in the eye.

"But this is crazy! Lana, don't torture me. I'm already hyperventilating. You *really* don't want him?"

Alana picked up the leatherbound menu, which was quite extensive. She studied it for a moment before answering. "As a husband, no; as my lifelong pal, yes. I'd be excited to be a god-mother, though. Maybe chief bridesmaid before that. Don't take any notice whatsoever of anything Vi says. She's a born trouble-maker, I'm afraid."

"You're telling me!" Rose huffed. "And Lil's just the same. It will blow up in their faces one day."

Simon was thrilled to have the opportunity of seeing Alana in the middle of his working day. He kissed her on both cheeks with Gallic aplomb, and smiled benignly on little Rose, who was looking remarkably pretty and flushed.

"Good lunch?" he asked, walking them to the parking lot.

"Great lunch!" both young women said together, then laughed.

"Well, the restaurant boasts a much-lauded chef," Simon pointed out with satisfaction. "What did you have?"

"Rose will tell you in the car." Alana lightly touched his arm. "She says you're driving her home?" Actually, Alana could easily have done that, but Rose obviously didn't want to miss out on a little private time with Simon.

"I wouldn't want her to drive after a few drinks," Simon said. "Our Rose can be quite naughty!"

"I like to enjoy myself, Simon, darling," said Rose, suddenly feeling free to take his arm. "We had a brilliant time." She puckered up to kiss Alana goodbye. "Just double-checking—you're entering The Naming, of course?" she asked. "Will I *ever* get a chance to shine? Everyone thinks I'm pretty cute, but *you're* something else again."

"I'm not entering, Rosie," Alana said firmly. "And I'm thinking it would be absolutely wonderful if *you* won."

"Truly? You want me to win?" Rose's big blue eyes widened.

Alana nodded. "I'll take loads of photos of you wearing the crown."

Simon, however, was searching Alana's face with a frown. "You're joking, aren't you, Lana?"

"No, Simon, I'm not,' she said sweetly, resisting the urge to pinch his cheek.

"But I've already entered you," Simon burst out, near broken-heartedly.

"You shouldn't have done that, Simon. It's my decision not to enter."

"Well, that's good news of a kind." Rose was looking on the bright side. "It gives the rest of us a chance."

Alana was walking, head down, to the ute, when a tall figure loomed up in front of her, his height blocking out the sunlight. "Hi," Guy said in a perfectly calm voice. "Lost in thought?"

She was glad her eyes were hidden behind the dark lenses of her sunglasses. "Why, hello, Guy. Is this the way it's going to be from now on?"

"And how's that?" He took her arm with unbearable gentleness and moved her into the shade of a trellis that was covered in a prolifically flowering white vine.

"We're not friends any more?"

"Were we ever friends?" he asked ironically, his dark eyes moving slowly over her.

She averted her head. "Maybe not. I've just had lunch with Rose."

"So I heard," he answered smoothly. "She thinks the world of you, Alana."

"And I'm very fond of Rose. It's Violette I like to keep a million miles from. Violette is still telling anyone who will listen Simon and I are two minutes from the altar. At least that's what Rose just told me."

He was looking at her white shirt, at the first three buttons undone, allowing a mere glimpse of the shadowed cleft between her breasts.

She felt she was burning alive, unable to lock out the memories of his hands on her.

"Well, I do hope you put her right!" he said.

Alana gave in to a wry laugh. "You should have seen her rush off with Simon. She told me about the job. She's thrilled. It's wonderful you're giving her a chance, Guy. It's what she needs. Rose is capable of so much more."

"I did it for *you*, Alana, as you well know," he returned bluntly.

"Excuse me?" She threw back her head, aglitter in the sunlight.

"Don't play dumb. It doesn't suit you in the least. I did what you suggested. I set it up so Rose and Simon are thrown together. I understood that's what you wanted?"

She heard the birds calling to one another, the bees droning, inhaled the nearly overpowering sweet scent of the cascades of white flowers. "Do you want me to go down on bended knee and thank you?"

He smiled. "Actually, that could be nice. Why don't I drive you home instead? It's damned hot, and I know for a fact the air conditioning in your ute has broken down."

"Is there anything you *don't* know? Anyway, there are such things as windows," she pointed out. She who had been forced to spend several minutes fixing her windblown hair when she'd arrived.

"If you could manage a smile, I'll get someone to fix it and deliver it back to the farm. Probably by tomorrow afternoon."

She would be a fool to turn such an offer down. "I can't let you do it, Guy."

"But you *can* let me play matchmaker to get Simon off your back?"

She smarted—just as he'd intended. "I love Simon."

"As a friend. Simon needs to be strong about recognising that fact. I'm sure Rose will do her very best to offer sympathy. I like Rose. As you say, there's so much more to her than she's been allowed to show. I think she can do this job, and do it well."

"So do I!" Her note was overly emphatic, as though he might change his mind. "She's ecstatic about it."

His mouth twitched. "I think she's more ecstatic about coming into daily contact with Simon. They're both gentle people. I need hardly say you're not!"

"Neither are *you!*" she shot back, affronted.

"You *are* going to let me drive you home, though?"

She stared up at him. "You're an intimidating man when you want to be, Guy Radcliffe."

He took her arm, leading her off to the reserved parking area, under shelter, where his car had pride of place. Once there, he opened the passenger door for her—but before she could make a move to slide into the leather seat he suddenly caught her chin, turned her face up to him and kissed her mouth.

She didn't know if it was fierce or tender or a combination of both, but her legs turned as wobbly as a toddler's.

"Lucky for you I'm not intimidating all the time," he said, placing a hand on the top of her head and guiding her down into the passenger seat as though she were his prisoner.

The countryside revealed itself in gentle swells of hill and dale, in every possible shade of green. Alana was very sensitive to all the different shades of nature. Graceful, broad-domed shade trees lined the valley road, and in the huge paddocks some species of wattle had already begun to burst into the glowing masses of golden blossom that outstripped the display turned on by the red and pink flowering gums.

Alana stared through the window of the gently purring car as the Valley landscape flashed by. The interior was beautifully cool. The top-of-the-range car was a far, far cry from the farm utility or indeed anything she was used to.

It was the bluest of blue days. A day to rejoice in—though if the truth be known numerous anxieties were tugging at her heart. A few shape-shifting white clouds were gathering over the hills. One looked like the dove of peace, with its wings outstretched. She didn't feel in the least peaceful. She was trying hard to resist the urge to touch her still pulsating mouth. Every kiss he gave her was more devastating than the last. If only she could read their *true* meaning. Tease away her doubts.

"Dad said such a strange thing to me before I left," she confided.

Guy glanced at her with a quick frown. "Oh? What?"

"He said he was going to see Father Brennan to make his confession."

Guy, being Guy, cut right to the heart of the matter. "What are you afraid of?"

"I believe Dad has a death wish." Her tone betrayed her sorrow.

"It's possible," Guy agreed quietly.

"Kieran and I are always on guard, but we can't be with him all the time."

"Where is Kieran today?"

She rested her head back. "He's gone over to the Mangans to give them a hand. Mr Mangan isn't properly on his feet after his operation."

"Yes, I know," Guy murmured, his mind clearly on other things. "You know your farm will have to go?"

She nodded in abject resignation. "Maybe you can give me a job, like Rose?" She heard the bitterness in her voice, then felt appalled by it. "I'm sorry. I know how that sounded."

"I could buy Briar's Ridge," Guy said.

She turned her head to look at him in amazement. He had sounded serious. "You don't need it."

"No."

"So why would you do it?"

A muscle clenched along his clean jawline. "I'd do it if it would get your father back on his feet." So she did mean something to him. But what?

"I don't believe it would," she answered, on reflection. "Dad is sunk in—not apathy, it's despair. He tried to make that 'confession' a joke but he can't fool me. He told me, 'There's love and there's *love.*' He said he'd let a dream rule his life. That he wasn't the one my mother wanted."

"Isn't *that* a confession?" Guy said with a strange note in his voice.

"You know it all, Guy. That's why I'm telling you. In a way, your family and mine are bound together The richest family in the Valley, descendants of the old squattocracy, and an Irish immigrant who arrived in this country as a penniless boy with only a kindly great-aunt to take him in. Why did my mother choose the man she did? Why did my mother choose my father when even my father believes he wasn't her heart's choice?"

Guy took his time before he answered. "Your mother was pregnant at the time of her marriage, Alana. She married the father of her child. It's as simple as that. She did what she believed was right."

Tears choked her throat. "Do we even know *that* for sure? Why do Kieran and Alex act so strangely whenever they see one another? If I didn't know better, I'd say Alex was Kieran's woman of mystery. She certainly looks the part. Maybe they think they're related? Maybe that's what they're afraid of?" She broke off, emotionally exhausted.

Guy's dark eyes cut to her distraught profile. "Alan Callaghan was the father of Annabel's child." His voice had the ring of certainty. "Don't make yourself sick toying with a fantasy. Although there *is* something odd in Kieran's relationship with my sister. Whatever it is, it's definitely not what you've just thrown in. You can get that out of your head right now. However your father won your mother—whatever method he used—it has haunted him. Believe me, Alana, Kieran is his son. Do you really think my father would have let his own child get away from him? Your mother alone made the decision to marry your father. She could not be dissuaded. Anyway, as a family you always gave the appearance of being happy. You *were* happy. Leave it at that, Alana. There's nothing to be gained by asking too many painful questions to which you might never get an answer."

Even so, immense frustration was building in her chest. "When I was a girl I used to hero-worship you," she said in a tight voice.

He kept his eyes on the road. "You said that with such a mix of emotions. Am I going to have to do battle for you, Alana? You know I want you. I'm having trouble thinking of anything else *but* wanting you." He lifted a hand off the wheel to touch her cheek.

Her body was swept by the sharpest aches and longings. *Don't you dare cry,* she admonished herself. But her feelings were reflected in the melancholy tone of her voice. "So we start an affair? Is that it? Because *you* want me? For how long? What happens when it's all over?" She turned her head to stare at him. "What could be the terrible result? For that matter, how do you know I won't trap you into marriage? Even for you, someone renowned for never making a mistake, it wouldn't be difficult. I could swear to be on the pill when I wasn't. It's been done before today. We both know of cases in the Valley."

"You could never trap me," he said. "The man who gets you, Alana, will be walking off with a prize. And let me correct you. I've made plenty of mistakes. Not, however, with women. Anyway, that's not the way you are. You don't have a dishonourable bone in your body."

"I hope not." Everything about him went deep with her. It was so much worse since they had crossed that dividing line. This man had the power to break her heart. She might be like her father. Some broken hearts never mended. "Do any of us truly know what we are until crisis time?" she asked. "Was Kieran's conception just an accident?"

Guy's face darkened. "Please, Alana, forget it."

"Easier said than done. Maybe much of life is a series of accidents? What do you really want of me, Guy? I must tell you I'm no plaything to be enjoyed and then thrown away."

"You think I see you as a plaything?" he asked with a flare of anger. "I don't fall into the emotionally screwed up category, Alana. And in case you've started thinking revenge; forget it. Revenge is not in my heart. We both know we've always had a connection, though I suppose both of us have done our best to cover it up. I was older when you were just growing up. It made a difference. *Then*."

Hadn't his position, his charisma, his experience and sophistication kept her in awe for a long time? She stared out of the window for a few moments. "Were you ever sleeping with Violette?" she asked finally. She couldn't stop herself. That was the other thing. His relationship with her cousin.

Guy's mouth twisted. "Okay—yes! I was for a while. I won't lie to you. My mother was very much in favor of Violette. I guess you don't understand why. I don't know that I do myself," he said wryly. "But Violette can be very charming when she puts her mind to it. She knows how to insinuate herself with the right people. I'm sure you know what I mean. But our relationship couldn't go beyond a certain stage. We're very different people. Violette will find someone to suit her. I've had plenty of girlfriends. You know that. Most of them are still my friends. I've never deliberately hurt a woman. The very *last* person I want to hurt is you."

"But despite your best intentions it could all turn out very differently," she said quietly. "If we became close, our differences might stand out.'

"Does that worry you?" he asked. "I've known you all your life, Alana. I haven't seen any essential differences. We're not opposite poles. We both love the land. Not everyone sees it as we do. We need this life. We love Nature. We feel its healing power."

"It hurts me to know you slept with Violette," she admitted. "Your affair—whatever it was—lasted quite a while. She must be good in bed."

A groan came from the back of Guy's throat. "Alana, even for you I can't kiss and tell. Did you want me to lie to you? Sex happens. I made no promises to Violette. I didn't lead her astray. We really weren't half as close as you seem to think. There's a thousand times more excitement in touching your cheek."

"So we're going to have a sexual relationship?" If so, she might lose herself for ever!

"That's what *I* want! I think we've gone past the stage where we can remain good friends."

"Would you like it if I said I've slept with Simon?"

He turned his head briefly. "No, I wouldn't," he said, unmistakably emphatic. "But you haven't. I'm thinking Simon *has* to be the Sir Galahad of the Valley. He adores you. It must have been very hard for him, treating you all this while as his best pal."

"He *is* my best pal, that's why!"

"What would I be, then?" He shot her a challenging glance. "Come on—tell me, so I'll know."

She began to count out on her fingers. "You're a man with a lot of influence. You have a lot of power. And, yes, you have loads and loads of money."

"Would you marry me for my money?"

"Of course I wouldn't. Anyway, I'm not thinking of marriage at this stage."

"What about six months from now?"

"You're fooling," she said shortly. She could see the sparkle in his eyes. "Go on, have your fun."

"You never know! Anyway, you and Simon are wrong for each other."

A little wave of sadness swept through her. "Simon is going to be dreadfully hurt."

"I know that, and I'm sorry. Simon is my cousin —he's *family*. But we both know Simon and Rose are much better suited. Besides, Rebecca will take a completely different view of Rose."

Alana gave a brittle laugh. "Rose is a Denby."

"So are you. Rebecca is an odd person," he commented unexpectedly.

"My mother used to say Rebecca 'wasn't quite right.'"

"And she was being kind. Keep away from Rebecca as much as possible."

She turned her head in surprise. "Why do you say that? Anyone would think I was considering moving in."

"Well—" Abruptly, Guy broke off what he'd been about to say. He further startled Alana by putting a warning hand on her arm. "Looks like there's been an accident up ahead. I can spot skid marks, and there's a gouge in that big tree that looks fresh. A vehicle might have skidded on the gravel, hit the tree, then flipped. We'll need to take a look."

Instantly Alana was riven by dread. Some part of her recognised that she had always been prepared for something like this. Her mother had lost her life not very far from here. Her father had told her he intended driving into town. That meant he would have had to travel this very road. Full-blown panic entered her bloodstream. The beauty of the day gave way to nightmare.

Guy stopped his car at the top of the rise, a few feet from the towering gum. An area of bark had been gouged out of the trunk, long strips of it lying around the base. Swiftly Guy got out of the car and came round to her. "Stay where you are. I can smell petrol."

She responded by trying to get out. "I'm coming too. You can't stop me."

"I can and I will," Guy said, looking grim and well capable of using force if he had to. "This is a dangerous situation, Alana. Stay put. You're needed to ring the police and an ambulance."

"Just tell me it's not our car," she implored, her hopes dimming.

Guy lifted his hand, then dropped it as if in futility. Despite himself he too was giving in to a peculiar dread. He moved off while Alana sat there, door open, making heartbreaking little keening sounds.

He was back to her in moments. "It *is* your car," he said, a world of regret in his voice. "I can see your father slumped over the wheel. The petrol fumes are strong. I have to get him out of there."

"But, Guy, the danger!" She stared up at him, wild-eyed. Could she lose Guy and her father too?

"I'll be fine," he insisted. "Just do what I tell you. Make those calls. There's no real help you can give. You'll only be in the way."

Urgently he moved down the woody slope. The smell of petrol was worrying him dreadfully. Alan Callaghan could be incinerated—a fate not to be borne. He was either unconscious or dead.

Guy reached the vehicle, tugging with all his might at the door handle. Finally he got it open. He reached in over Alan Callaghan's dark head to turn off the ignition, his heart flipping at the moan that issued from the injured man's throat.

Thank God!

Guy withdrew his head for a split second, shouting back to Alana, who was standing at the lip of the slope, staring down at the crash scene. "He's alive!" *But in what condition?*

Blood was running from a wound high up on Alan Callaghan's temple. Working swiftly, fearing the situation, Guy

released the seat belt, then got his arm around the man. There
was no way he could leave Alan Callaghan where he was. The
car could catch fire at any minute. It would explode. Too
gruesome a death! One to be avoided at all costs. There was
nothing else for it but to carry the semi-conscious man up the
slope. To Guy's immense relief, Alan Callaghan roused himself,
then made a definite effort to stand on his own two feet.

"I've got you, Alan!" Guy cried. "We have to get up the
slope as quickly as we can."

Just as he had done once before, Guy slung his arm around
the big man, half pulling, half dragging him up the slope,
which mercifully wasn't steep.

Oh, Dad—Dad, what's to become of you? Alana shook her
head, her nerves raw. Was this an attempted suicide? Or had
her father simply lost control of the vehicle when he'd skidded
on the gravel? Going on the strength of the petrol fumes, she
was terrified he and Guy wouldn't make it up the slope until
it was too late. And she was in danger herself, standing so
close to the lip. But she couldn't bring herself to move away.

I can't face life without these two.

If anything bad happened now it would break her. There
had been so many losses, her spirit would simply call it quits.

"There's a rug in the boot," Guy called to her. "Be quick,
Alana. Get it and drape it over the back seat. I'll put your
father there. We can get him to hospital much faster than
waiting for the ambulance."

Alana ran.

Less than a few minutes after that, with Guy's car speeding
back towards the town, the Callaghan's car exploded. It went
up in a solid wall of orange flame, with sections of buckled
steel flying like missiles through the sulphurous air.

CHAPTER SEVEN

THEY were sitting in the waiting room, hoping for news of Alan Callaghan's condition.

Alana knew she would have been locked into a dark world if Guy hadn't been with her. His strong, calm presence lent her tremendous support. He was, in fact, holding her hand. She didn't know when he had taken it, but she wasn't going to let go. Some time in the future, when her father had made it, she was going to thank Guy for saving her father's life. It had been a very brave thing to do. Not everyone would have taken such a risk. Most people would have been thinking, quite naturally, of their own survival. Now her mind was dulled with shock, replaying the incident over and over, trying to fathom what had been in her father's mind. She was leaning against Guy, her head resting on his shoulder, but she was no longer fully conscious of what she was doing.

"Lana?"

They both looked up as Kieran, with a visibly upset Buddy in tow, came into the waiting room. News of the crash had travelled with the speed of lightning. It had reached the Mangan farm in no time at all.

Alana stood up, throwing herself into her brother's arms. They closed around her powerfully, conveying the state Kieran was in, but there was a faintly bitter edge to his voice. "What's all this about, Lana?" he asked, his handsome face pinched. "Was it an accident, or Dad deciding to call it a day?"

She could only murmur helplessly, "I don't know. I don't know."

"Well, the police will soon sort it out," Kieran said grimly. "God, I'll have to stop Buddy blubbing. It's really getting to me."

Alana looked towards the sobbing youngster. "He loves Dad."

"Well, I love Dad too, but I'm fed up with all this. What was in Dad's mind? Doesn't he care about *us* at all? Doesn't he care how we would feel *afterwards?*"

Clearly Kieran thought it was a failed suicide attempt.

Guy, on the other hand, was by no means sure of that. He decided to intervene. Alana looked pale enough to faint. "It could well have been an accident, Kieran," he said, joining them.

"Or Dad determined on taking his last ride," Kieran said in a choked voice. "We can't thank you enough, Guy. You're a hero."

"Forget that!" Guy brushed all mention of heroism aside. "I did what you would have done in the same circumstances."

"You're a hero in my book," Kieran repeated firmly, suddenly turning on the weeping Buddy. "For goodness' sake, Buddy, quit it!" It was obvious he was in no mood to listen to Buddy's choking sobs, which had started the very minute they got the news.

Guy twisted about to get an arm around Buddy's slight shoulders. "You've got to be strong now, Buddy. Think you can do it?"

"I'm a bit of a mess right now, Mr Radcliffe," Buddy said pitifully.

"We *all* are, Buddy. But we mustn't slip into despair."

Buddy rolled his eyes. "You were willin' to go down to a rolled car that was threatenin' to blow up! I call that mighty brave."

Incredibly brave, Alana thought.

"It wasn't about bravery, Buddy," Guy said, finding being

labelled brave a burden. "It was doing what had to be done. Now, let's forget it."

I'll never forget it! Alana thought.

Minutes later Simon and Rose hurried in, both showing their concern. "When we first heard there had been an accident Simon nearly went off his head," Rose confided to Alana quietly. "We had absolutely no idea at that point it was your father. Simon thought it was you. Maybe there's a lesson to be learned in that. He loves *you,* Lana. Only you."

Alana looked into Rose's blue eyes. "He's there for me, Rosie as I'll always be there for him. Oh, look—" her gaze went past her cousin "—it's Dr Pitman."

They all rose to their feet. They all knew Bill Pitman, who was in his early fifties and had a shock of pure white hair. He was the hospital's cardiologist and head of the emergency team.

"Okay," Pitman announced briskly, but with sympathy and understanding. "Alan has had a heart attack. It was that which caused him to lose consciousness at the wheel. Our immediate goal has been to ease his pain and discomfort. Now we have to clear the blocked coronary artery and restore blood-flow to the heart." He turned to Guy. "Only you acting so quickly, getting him to the hospital in time, Guy, after pulling him out of the car, has ensured his survival. I won't beat about the bush. Alan is a sick man. We all know he hasn't been looking after himself. I'm going to keep him here for a day or so. I want to run more tests. He'll need bypass surgery, so be prepared for that."

"Can we see him?" Alana asked, experiencing a degree of relief that it had been an accident and not attempted suicide.

"For a moment only." Bill Pitman smiled gently. "You and Kieran. Your father is groggy. He needs to be kept quiet."

"Of course." Guy, who had saved Alan Callaghan's life, nodded his head on behalf of the rest of them.

The fact it had been an accident made quite a difference,

Guy thought. He could see the relief neither Alana nor Kieran
was able to keep out of their faces. Bypass surgery had a high
success rate. With the proper care Alan Callaghan had many
more years of life left. What he had to do was make huge
change to his lifestyle. That was if he really wanted to live.

Alan Callaghan's quadruple bypass was scheduled for ten
days' time. He was sent home on medication. There was no
question of his touching alcohol. Alana was certain he'd make
no attempt to, even when no one was around. Not that he was
left on his own for any length of time. Kieran was managing
the farm almost single-handedly. She devoted her time to her
father watching him like a hawk, and when she took a short
break Buddy, who had moved into the house from the cottage,
was at hand.

"A man's never alone for five minutes!" Alan Callaghan
pretended to growl. "Can't even go to the lavatory on my
own." It was true Buddy followed him there, on sentry duty
outside the door.

The Wine Festival Dinner-Dance was to take place on the
Saturday night, but Alana had no thought of going. She had
to be home with her father. She was going to be extremely
nervous until he had his operation, and stood over him while
he took his medication. Simon came over frequently—mostly
to see Alana, but genuinely concerned for her father's health.

"Surely Buddy can watch your dad for a few hours?" he
suggested. "He looks all right to me. In fact much better." That
at least was true.

"There will be other dinner-dances, Simon," she said.
"Take Rose. You and she have been spending a bit of time
together, I hear."

"Bless her. She's been a big help when I'm really busy,"
Simon said quite fondly. "It's just as you said. There's a lot
more to Rose than meets the eye."

"Gosh, I would have thought what meets the eye was good enough for most guys," Alana said. "Maybe Rose is having a calming influence on you? As for me—one part of me is really sorry I'm missing out, the other knows where love and duty lie."

But her father when he found out, wouldn't hear of her missing out on the big night. "Alana, I won't sleep until you tell me you're going. I'm as right as rain, my girl. Haven't you been noticing how much better I am? Would you deprive your father of the pleasure of seeing you all dressed up and winning The Naming? Think about it. I'd be far happier seeing you go off to the ball than seeing you sitting home with me. I can watch some television. Buddy will keep me company. Buddy's perfectly capable of keeping an eye on me. As if I need it! I can't have you worrying yourself sick about me. I *want* you to go."

Alana had a problem. She didn't have a dress.

Kieran worked close to the homestead while Alana took a quick trip into town. There were two excellent boutiques. Maybe she could find something to fit her budget?

She was coming out of the first boutique, having tried on several lovely but too expensive garments, intending to move on to another shop to check out what they had in stock, when a well-bred but severe-sounding voice hailed her.

"You're going to the dinner-dance, then, Alana?"

Alana spun to look into Rebecca Radcliffe's obsidian eyes. Of all the rotten luck! "Oh, hello, Mrs Radcliffe." Hastily she put a smile on her face. "Dad doesn't want me to miss out."

"How is he?" Rebecca asked, with little show of concern.

"Much better, thank you." Alana moved into the arcade for privacy. Rebecca followed suit. "He's due to have a bypass on the fourteenth."

Rebecca smiled thinly. "I know. My son tells me everything. I'm not quite sure what it is you want from my son, Alana. Perhaps, since we're on our own, you can enlighten me?"

Alana knew a challenge when she heard it. She began a slow count to ten. "Mrs Radcliffe, Simon and I have been friends since we first started carrying school bags. Friends are what we are. I thought that was understood."

"Oh, please." Rebecca gave a nasty little jeer. "You know, I can't figure you out, Alana. You don't want my son, yet you can't bear to let him go. You give him no chance to be with other girls, you demand his constant attention, and all the time you have your eye on Guy. No, don't attempt to deny it. I'm no fool. Guy's one of your little secrets, isn't he? You've been infatuated with him for years now. I remember as if it were yesterday you looking up at him at your eighteenth birthday. I remember his kissing your cheek. I remember how you touched it afterwards. A dead give-away to anyone watching, as I was. Guy, of course, has an understanding with your cousin, Violette. You know that. But I suppose a girl can dream. You won't get him, my dear. Though I suppose he can't help being fascinated. You *are* beautiful. A heartbreaker, like your mother. But you won't get Guy, mark my words. There's bad blood there."

Alana wasn't as profoundly shocked as she once would have been. Nevertheless, she felt as though an arrow had pierced her heart. She stared back at Rebecca's face, with its fine, cold features, for the longest time. "How dare you attempt to defile my mother's memory?" she said, her voice low and vibrating with emotion. "I'd have a care, if I were you. Someone might start dragging out *your* secrets, and I bet you've got a few. What are you talking about anyway? Bad blood?" The anger that was in her showed in her sparkling eyes.

Rebecca Radcliffe gave another one of her thin, hateful smiles. "You're such a passionate creature, aren't you?" She made it sound like a serious character defect. "I know when to keep my mouth shut. There's plenty that has been kept hidden. Plenty that has been kept within the family. *I'm* family. You forget, I was married to David Radcliffe's brother."

Alana's Irish temper unfortunately got the better of her. "Who seemed pretty desperate to get away from you," she shot back, then immediately apologised. "I'm sorry, I shouldn't have said that. But I can't stand here being insulted by you, Mrs Radcliffe. I've been through a pretty emotionally worrying time with my father. I won't let you upset me further, though upsetting people *is* your specialty. If you've got concerns about Simon and me, speak to Simon. Personally, I think Simon's big problem in life is *you!*"

That was all wrong, she fumed, as she rushed away. But didn't Rebecca deserve it? Alana didn't want to look at dresses any more. She didn't want to go to the dinner-dance. Thoroughly upset, she kept on walking, past where she had intended to go and on to where she had parked the ute. What a dreadful woman Rebecca was. No wonder Simon lacked backbone, with a mother like that to drive him crazy. Alana was doing Rose a huge disservice, pushing her in Simon's direction. Razor-tongued Violette was much better suited to dealing with a potential mother-in-law like Rebecca.

She had almost made it back to the ute when Guy, who was driving through town spotted her bright head. It really was a beacon, that mane, he thought—not for the first time. There was a parking spot just behind the utility. He pulled into it, getting out of the car and greeting her across the bonnet. "So—what are you doing in town?"

Her heart did its usual flip. This love of mine, she thought. This *secret* love of mine. "I haven't been here for long," she said, the tremble in her voice betraying her agitation. "I ran into Simon's mother."

"Aaah!" Guy expelled a long understanding breath, joining her on the pavement. "That must have been like running into an iceberg. So, what did she say?"

Alana put a hand to her temple. "Let's see. Where shall I start?"

"Come and have a cup of coffee with me," he said. "You can tell me then."

"I should get home to Dad."

"Coffee will give you a kick. We won't be long." He took her arm. "Actually, I wanted to suggest getting a trained nurse in to watch him this weekend. You are coming to the function?"

"I wasn't." She allowed herself to be steered towards the town's newest and by far best bistro, run by an Italian family, newcomers to the district. They had turned an ordinary little café that had been losing money into a thriving business. The coffee was everything coffee should be, the light meals were delicious, and the specialty breads, the luscious little tarts, slices, mouth-watering cheesecakes, were all made on the premises by different members of the family.

"So, what changed your mind? Guy asked.

"Dad persuaded me. That's what I was doing in town. I was after a dress."

"Why don't you let Alex pick a couple out for you in Sydney?" he suggested, as if that was the perfect solution. "She'd know exactly what would suit you."

"I'm certain she would. Alex has superb taste. But perhaps I should tell you I'm on a budget." Of course the Radcliffes didn't know what budgets *were*. They had millions.

"I'm sure Alex could find you something ridiculously cheap and gorgeous at the same time," Guy said smoothly. "She'd love to help out. You won't find what you're looking for here."

"Most women aren't prepared to pay *astronomical* prices for dresses," she pointed out. "Anyway, I'm not going."

"Yes, you are," he coolly contradicted. "Personally, I'd be shocked if you didn't win the title of most beautiful girl in the Valley wearing something run up from a hessian bag."

Guy opened the glass-paned door of the bistro, allowing Alana to step into the relaxed charm of a large open room, decorated very much in the Italian style. The lunchtime wave was over—the bistro had been packed—so there were tables available. The grandfather of the family, Aldo—a big man, slightly overweight, still handsome in his early seventies, with warm, expressive brown eyes and a head of tightly furled white curls—hurried over to greet them, shepherding them happily towards the best table available.

They settled on the same thing. A slice of *timballo,* a marvellous home made chicken and mushroom pie in a pasta case. "And Mamma has made her famous hazelnut and chocolate cake," Aldo confided, as though no one could possibly resist.

Alana looked up to smile. "Then I can't say no."

Guy gave a relaxed nod. "I won't say no either, Aldo." He'd had nothing since seven o'clock that morning. He didn't normally stop for lunch, preferring to wait for dinner. "A glass each of one of your good dry whites with the *timballo,* one long black with the chocolate cake, and—what?—a cappuccino for you, Alana?"

"Perfect," she sighed, realising not only how hungry she was but what wonderful restorative powers even the mention of food had. She recalled how her mother had adored reading cookbooks.

"Have you heard from your granddaughter?" Guy asked pleasantly, watching Aldo's face light up with love and pride. Daniela Adami, at twenty-six, had worked with famous chefs in Paris and Rome. Guy had learned at present she was sous chef to the executive chef at a famous London hotel. The entire family were excellent cooks, but Daniela had taken things to an even higher level. She was a young *cordon bleu,* fast making a name for herself.

"She rang only last night," Aldo told them. "She's well and happy, but she's missing the family. She's been away from us for nearly five years now. Always climbing the ladder. One of these days she'll come home and open her own restaurant. She is a *real* chef, our Daniela. Even the male chefs don't mind taking orders from her in the kitchen. She's as good with people as she is with food. We sent her back to Europe to learn, but there's so much happening here in Australia. Great Australian chefs. Great Australian restaurants. Marvellous ingredients—ah, the sea food! Nothing short of superb!" He kissed the tips of his fingers. "We must pay homage to the great chef you have at your estate restaurant, Mr Radcliffe."

"Why don't you and your wife visit on Saturday night?" Guy suggested, knowing other members of the family would keep Aldo's restaurant going. "I'll arrange for a table. You'll come as my guests. Who knows? Daniela might one day bring her culinary art to Wangaree Valley."

Aldo burst into a flood of lyrical Italian, raising his hand over them like a priest giving a blessing.

"You've made his day," Alana commented, as Aldo moved off to attend to their order.

"I like this family." Guy looked around him. "They're good for the town. I want them to fit in."

"I think they already have."

Thirty leisurely minutes later, they were walking back to their cars. "Feeling better?" asked Guy.

"Much," Alana said, visibly perked up. "Simon's mother is such an upsetting woman. She goes out of her way to be unpleasant. How did she come to have a sensitive, gentle son like Simon?"

Guy shrugged. "One of life's great mysteries."

"I pity the woman he ends up marrying," Alana said, looking up at Guy with a frown. "I think we've done entirely the wrong thing, trying to set him up with Rose."

"It must have slipped your attention that a girl like Rose wouldn't offer Rebecca any challenge. You, on the other hand, do. Rose will know how to handle Rebecca. She's by no means as empty headed as she acts."

"Empty-headed?" Alana looked at him aghast. "I don't believe you said that."

"Just an observation. Let me rephrase it. Rose, however pretty, comes across as a little vapid when compared with you."

"Damn it, Guy, *you* gave her a job!"

"Of course I did. It's as I said. She's pretty. She's friendly. People like her. And she's been given the opportunity to prove she's a lot smarter than people give her credit for. I like Rose—I *do*. We get along well. Besides, it's only my opinion."

Alana broke into a wry laugh. "Lord only knows what your real opinion of me is, then."

He glanced down on her head. "I can't lie. You'd be flattered." He used the remote to open his car. "Hop in for a moment," he said, his hand on the passenger side door. "I have something I want to discuss with you. Won't take a minute."

"Why so mysterious?' she asked, feeling more and more exposed the closer she got to him.

"Hop in," he repeated.

"Whether I like it or not," Alana muttered, doing as she was told.

A moment later Guy slipped into the driver's seat beside her, all radiant male energy, completely in charge of himself. *And her.*

"I wanted to get your reaction first." He turned to her, his dark eyes signalling serious business. "I know someone who would very much like to buy into the Valley. His family has been long established in the New England area. They own and run a well-known sheep station, Gilgarra."

"Of course I've heard of it," Alana said.

"Yes, well, I went to school and university with Linc, but he has an older brother. He wants a place of his own. He never did get on with his father anyway. I don't think Alan would have any difficulty selling Linc Briar's Ridge for a good price."

Alana sat clutching her handbag in her lap. Her face

showed a whole range of emotions. "You've gone ahead and discussed it with this Linc?" she asked.

"I'm discussing it with *you,* Alana. Linc is a good friend of mine. I know his ambitions."

"Linc who?" Her beautiful hazel eyes were throwing off sparks. "What's their name again?"

"Linc Mastermann," he said calmly. "His first name is actually Carl. His mother was Barbara Lincoln, of the Victorian pastoral family. Somewhere along the line Carl got to be Linc."

Alana looked straight ahead of her. She wanted to stop this conversation, but knew that she should listen. The farm had to go. They all knew that. Even if it weren't so deeply in the red, and her father's bypass operation was a great success, she wouldn't want her father returning to a life of hard physical work.

"I'm sorry, Alana," Guy said, giving her a tender look she missed. "I know how much you love your home."

"And what about the horses? And my dogs?" she burst out emotionally, turning her head accusingly, as though it were all his fault.

"You won't have a problem finding the dogs a good home. I'll even take them myself. And Linc would want to keep the horses. It's not the time to talk to your father yet, though. He simply isn't well enough to handle it. I've spoken to Kieran, of course."

"Of course!" Her tone held bitterness. "Let the *men* settle it!"

"It's not that at all." His own tone turned terse. "Kieran has been living a life that doesn't altogether suit him. He's an artist. He's only just come to the realisation he could be very, very good. Kieran won't have a big problem making the transition to a different lifestyle."

She knew that was probably true, yet she was filled with a boundless sense of loss. She put her hands to her head. It seemed to be spinning. "And what about me?" She was determined to hold back the tears. "I love this life. I don't want to go off to the city. Work in an office. Hemmed in. I don't want that."

He leaned towards her, his voice deep and soothing. "Don't get angry. I'm not suggesting that at all. Why don't we take one thing at a time, Alana? Your father's operation first, and then we must give him time to recuperate. All I'm saying is I have a buyer for when the time comes. At least I can take that worry off your mind. The sale could be handled smoothly and privately. I'll do everything I can to make that happen."

The tenderness in his voice, the sheer seductiveness of it, quite undid her. "And what do you get out of this, Guy?" she demanded, throwing out an emotional challenge. "What do *you* get out of it?"

His eyes were brilliant with intensity. "I get *you.*"

"Me?" Her voice broke.

"You," he repeated, taking hold of her nerveless hand, straightening out her curled-over fingers, exercising the power he had over her. "We started out talking business. Let's stick to that. It's time I married. I want a wife who can be many things, and I believe you can easily fill that role. You can give me what I want and need. That definitely includes children at some future time. As for me, I can give you security and the right environment to blossom. I don't like seeing you work so hard, Alana. You're young now, so you're not feeling it as much as you should. You won't always want to work a six-day week. I want to look after you. I want you to look after me. Both of us can look after Wangaree. I don't just want a beautiful wife, I want a full partner. I want a woman I can talk to about everything. I don't even mind if she wants to fight me from time to time."

"And you think *I* can handle all that?" she erupted.

"I *know* you can."

"So what about love? L-O-V-E?" She spelled it out. "Oh, Guy!" She moaned as though her heart was breaking. "Do you want love at *all?*"

His long fingers suddenly laced into her thick golden hair, turning her face to him. "I want everything you can offer me," he said.

CHAPTER EIGHT

KEIRAN saw her sleek car picking up speed as it moved away from the homestead and down the gravelled drive. So she didn't intend to stick around to say hello to him? The more fiercely he wanted her, the less it worked. He was desperately close to deciding to put half a world between them. Would he *never* get rid of the feelings of remorse, the sadness of it all, the loss? Even that hadn't separated them. The two of them were locked in the most passionate of hells.

He knew she had brought Alana a dress to wear for the big function tonight. The whole Valley was *en fête*. He wasn't going. He couldn't bear to see her there, an impossibly beautiful orchid on the shoulder of that oaf Roger Westcott. Westcott wasn't going away. Westcott would grow old before he let Alex go. He wanted her, and he was prepared to hang in there for as long as it took. Forget Westcott. Think Sidonie Radcliffe. Sidonie and her party of socialites were staying at Wangaree for the gala weekend. He couldn't bear to come into contact with the great Sidonie Radciffe. He'd sooner be thrown into a cellar full of snakes.

His expression softened as he thought of Alana. She would be certain to win the crown of most beautiful girl in the Valley. But her own family wouldn't be around her. Their adored mother was gone. Their father has a mere shadow of what he had once been. Keiran was terribly worried about their father. Everyone kept telling him the operation had a high success rate, but did their father have any positive feelings left to pull him through? Of course the ever faithful Simon—who was a nice guy, but kind of gutless—would be there to partner Alana. Alana had had numerous admirers over the years she'd never seemed to take any notice of. It hurt to be deprived of the pleasure of seeing his beautiful sister in the Naming. His own Dark Lady was too perfect to be allowed to enter. It wasn't nice, her driving away; it was oddly out of character. She knew how badly he would want to see her. He kicked the gelding into a gallop.

She saw him coming, riding hell for leather down the steep slope. He and Alana were splendid riders. Not many could touch them. Guy. Violette Denby, a few others. There was beauty in Violette, but malcontent marred it. He was coming so fast that for a heart-stopping moment she thought he was going to gather his mount and fly over the sloping hood of her car as if he was clearing a jump. Swiftly she pulled off the unsealed road, nosing into the shade of a feathery acacia. Nerves jingling, she turned off the engine and lowered the passenger window—ready to confront him, but with some protection. Not that he had ever, or would ever, physically hurt her, but on occasion he had a very tough persona.

He reined in a few feet away, dismounted, then looped the reins around a low branch of the tree, trying to calm himself to no avail.

"Get out of the car," he said. There was urgency and anger in his taut handsome face. "Get out of the car, Alex," he repeated, blue eyes blazing.

It was useless to defy him. She stood out of the car, head bent, her slender shoulders faintly slumped.

He hauled her right into his arms, his chin coming down

hard on her gleaming head. "You weren't going to wait and say hello to me?" he accused her, with burning intensity.

She threw up her head, inching it back so she could stare into his face. "Sometimes I can't take what you do to me, Kieran." There was such a sad and haunted look in her beautiful dark eyes it would have melted a heart of stone.

"You think it's easier for *me?*" He locked his steely arms around her, staring down into her face with an expression that bordered on anguish. "I've tried and tried to blot out our past, but something—God, what is it? Conscience?—won't let me. All I know is despite what you did to us, I have a boundless hunger for you. I can't think it will ever be assuaged."

He gave way to his longing and brought his mouth down over hers, a driven man, covering it in a furious kiss that plunged him into white-hot arousal. Her hold over him was so powerful, was it any wonder it struck fear into him?

"When am I going to see you? How?" He rubbed his thumb up and down her white throat. "I *have* to be with you."

She too was engulfed, trying hard to speak. "Maybe you should do something drastic and start afresh. Things don't have to be the way they are, Kieran. We've wasted so much of our lives. We've sought what we want in others, but neither of us could ever find it. We're no good together. No good apart. There has to be an end to it. We have to break out of the prison." She lifted her head. "Alana told me you've decided not to come tonight?"

He let his hand cup her breast, openly claiming it. "And watch you from a distance?" He gave a rasping laugh. "Watch that fool Westcott drool all over you? He never takes his eyes off you. How often have you claimed you were going to marry him? Why haven't you? You're just trying to torture me, that's all. Anyway, do you think I would go with your mother there?"

She moaned. "Oh, Kieran, you're so hard on us all. Please don't start on my mother again."

"She started on *me*. I was the boy from the wrong side of the tracks with a sword in his heart." Tears stung the back of his eyes. Darkness surrounded all his thoughts of Sidonie Radcliffe. Such was the drama of the past he had become so traumatised he couldn't speak of certain things. It was as though that woman had sewn his lips shut.

"*Don't*, Kieran!" Alex shook her head so violently the soft knot at her nape came loose, sending her hair swirling down her back. "You've stuck to your belief she forced me into having an abortion. I've told you in vain it didn't happen. My mother didn't even know until afterwards. No one knew I was pregnant but you, me and Dr Moreton."

"Who, conveniently, is long dead," Kieran said, the chaos of it all still in his head.

Alex was well beyond frustration. This had gone on too long. It had all but wrecked their lives. "I've told you and told you—Dr Moreton would never have consented to performing an abortion, or steering me to some other doctor who would. I *wanted* our precious child, even if we were hardly more than kids ourselves. We could have handled the situation with a little help. As it is, neither of us can move on. We can't be happy together. We can't be happy apart. I should hate you for it, because it's *you*, Kieran, who is driven to punish us both."

Tragically, there was truth in that. "Do you think I *want* to be the way I am?" He pulled her to him, staying very quiet for a moment. "I'll always have the death of our baby on my conscience, Alex. I can't help it. It's my nature. For years I had nightmares about it. I even made drawings of our child inside your womb, as though the pictures could help me communicate with it. I've had lost children hidden in my paintings. *You've* seen them, if no on else can. I'm not an uncaring man. The trouble is I care too much. You say we could have managed? We could have managed with *my* parents. *Your* parents would never have allowed it, no matter what you say. They couldn't have coped with the disgrace. Their beautiful only daughter pregnant by a nobody? That was how your mother saw me. I could never be a fitting partner for you."

"That's ridiculous, Kieran," she said fiercely, at the same time knowing he was right about her mother. "You're a very *special* person. Only you're unbelievably stubborn. You believe what you choose to believe." She lifted a hand, hit it helplessly against his chest. "We've battled this for years and years. Why?" She struck him again. "You've condemned me for having an abortion without your knowledge or approval. The truth is as I told you from the beginning. I had a miscarriage."

He pinioned her arms. "Please stop, Alex. It does no good."

Pain twisted like a knife inside her. "You can't think *Guy* knew?"

"I accept Guy didn't know," he answered quietly. "Guy was away at university most of the time. In any event, he would have stood by you."

Every word rained on her like a fresh blow. "Where have our dreams gone, Kieran?" she asked tragically. "You can't live without me, even though you've branded me a liar. And I love you, God help me. I've always loved you—only you. But I can go on like this any more. I want children. *Your* children. But you deny me."

There was such a glitter in his brilliant blue eyes. "It wouldn't be the same, though, would it? We ended one life."

Before she could stop herself her hand flashed up, cracking across his cheek. "Stop it, Kieran!" she cried. Blood was rushing in and out of her heart. "*Stop it!* I want the pain lifted. I want an end to the nightmare. I want someone to love me unconditionally. I want to be a *mother.*" She twisted away from him violently, making a dive into her car.

Kieran gave way to remorse. "Alex, don't go." He held the door fast.

"I must. Please stand away from the car, Kieran," she said with hard determination. "You have to let me go."

"It's too late for that. You're the pattern of my life." He continued to stare down at her. "I've thought of going far away. Travelling halfway across the world to forget you, let both of us get on with our lives, but I know in my heart the world isn't big enough."

Slowly he shut the car door. Alex switched on the ignition, put the car into reverse, and once on the road drove away swiftly, sending dust and debris flying out from the spinning wheels.

She was weeping.

Kieran could hear his own agitated breathing. His tears had to remain silent, unshed. They fell, as they had fallen for so many years now, down the walls of his heart. Alex never lied, but in this one desperate instance she *had*. She had never changed her story—perhaps understandably blinding herself to her shame and her guilt. He knew she *had* had an abortion, though he had never told her his unimpeachable source. A few times he had come desperately close. But he had sworn an oath to Alex's mother he wouldn't. She had insisted it be a binding oath. He was not to tell Alex. *Ever.* Alex had to be left alone to grapple with her own grief. She had made the decision. She had thought it the only one open to her. Maybe she had believed life as she wished to live it would have been drastically altered had she borne his child?

Only his child had had a right to life. That fact took precedence over every other consideration. They could have weathered the storm together. In all likelihood the storm would have passed over quickly. But Alex had failed them both. She had made an irreversible decision. Her choice. Her own mother had admitted it, sobbing brokenheartedly as she did so. Mothers didn't lie. The loss of a grandchild, she had told him, was a tragic event, the cruellest thing. She too suffered. She had wanted him, her daughter's seducer, to be very aware of that. But Alex alone had made the decision. He had to live with it. Moreover, they had to break up. He had done enough damage to her beautiful daughter.

From that day on he knew he had made a powerful enemy in Sidonie Radcliffe. The great irony of it was some of the time he didn't even blame her. He was the one, after all, who had got Alex pregnant.

Parental love blazed out of Alan Callaghan's face as he looked at his daughter, twirling before him. She was wearing a long gauzy gold dress that made her look extraordinarily radiant. He was quite certain she would win the title of the most beautiful girl in the Valley, as her mother had before her. He decided there and then that from now on he was going to do his very best to get back on his feet. He had given not only himself but his children hell. Time now to throw off despair. Father Brennan had talked sense to him, as he always had. And he would have his operation. He had been told he should come through it well. And he would stop drinking. He had never really liked the taste of whisky anyway. It was only to keep his heart and mind still. He would have to sell Briar's Ridge, but maybe the farm held too many unquenchable memories.

Guy had told him he would do everything he could to help him. What a man was he? Guy had to know Alan had once stolen the much-loved Annabel Derby from his own father.

He and David Radcliffe had had one thing in common. Both of them had been madly, irrevocably, in love with Annabel. That was how the split between David and Annabel had come about. Alan had been waiting—with some cunning, he had to admit—in the wings, ready to step into whatever little void opened up. Annabel's anger with David—they had fought about *him;* David had been right to be jealous—had not burnt itself out. Pride had kept David away overlong. The proud and high-spirited Annabel had been looking for comfort. Alan Callaghan had provided it, overcoming her in the end, but never forcibly. That one night—magical for him—had been consensual. Hadn't it? He'd been a fine-looking guy in those days. He knew if there hadn't been a David Radcliffe Annabel would have let herself fall in love with *him*. For one night the world of the senses had swallowed them up. They'd been young. Hot-blooded. Kieran had been conceived.

So be it!

Now Alana, arms extended, danced before him, looking the image of her mother. He whispered her name. *"Annabel!"*

"It's me, Dad." Alana broke off her twirling, sending him a poignant glance. She moved to where her father was sitting, in his favourite armchair, his face illuminated with pride. She bent down to kiss him lovingly on his cheek. "So, what do you think. A front runner?" She tried to joke, but her heart wasn't in it. Kieran was staying at home with their father, so she wouldn't have to worry about him, but she had been carrying countless nagging anxieties all day.

"A clear winner!" Her father gave her the thumbs up.

"Belle of the ball!" Kieran said, truly affected by his sister's beauty. "You look ravishing. That's one helluva dress, I can tell you. It suits you perfectly."

"I have to thank Alex for that." Alana smiled at him, conscious her brother was in as much inner turmoil as she was. "She has exquisite taste."

"Sure!" Kieran shrugged laconically. "I won't ask how much it cost."

Alana pulled a little face. "I think Alex fibbed about that."

Kieran glanced away. Twice he had picked up the phone to call her. Twice he had put the phone down. The only place he could have her to himself was in Sydney. He had put Alex under enormous pressure for too many years now. Unless he could set the spirit of their lost child free he would destroy her. And with her, himself. Like his father, he had to change.

* * *

Alana was conscious as she and Simon entered the glittering restaurant and threaded their way through to their allotted table that everyone was smiling at her.

"See—you're the favourite!" Simon snorted with pride. "Told you so!"

An old friend of her mother's caught her fingers. "Don't you let us down now, Lana," she whispered cosily, thinking but not saying, because that would be too emotional, how she wished Alana's mother could have been there.

So I'm expected to be Named? Alana thought, sliding gracefully into the cushioned chair Simon pulled out for her. Most of the tables, apart from the main table where the judging committee was seated, were set for ten, with floor-length tablecloths and napkins, seat cushions as well, in alternating colours of soft pink and yellow that lifted the room, with all its dark polished timber, and made it glow. Glass bowls of glorious pink and yellow roses adorned the centre of each table, with tapering white candles set to either side. The huge room had taken on a decidedly glamorous air—a fitting setting for this gala function. Whoever was responsible for it had done a splendid job.

Rose arrived, looking marvellously pretty in hyacinth-blue, which that drew attention to her eyes. She greeted everyone happily, looking down at her dinner card. "Oh, look—I'm next to you, Simon," she said, as though it were a big surprise instead of scrupulously planned. "Lana! You look like a film star—seriously *sexy!*" she announced, eyes wide. She had never seen so much of her cousin's yummy figure. Alana had such a beautiful bust. She should show it more often. "Where did you get that dress?" she demanded to know. "Violette will be *livid!*"

Alana smiled sweetly. "Sorry, I can't tell you. It's a secret."

"It's to die for!" Rose let her expert eyes move over her

cousin's shimmering silk organza strapless gown. "Believe me, you're going to win!"

Alana tried not to laugh. "It's not a matter of life and death, Rosie."

"It is to Violette!" Rose hissed from behind her hand.

Heads turned, as Alex rose from the main table to come over and say hello. She looked exquisitely beautiful, in a décolleté white gown with big South Sea pearls hanging from her ears, and another large pearl on a long shaft appended to a glittering white-gold chain around her throat.

She greeted everyone around the table, exchanged a few pleasantries, then spoke quietly to Alana as everyone turned back to their own conversation. "You look wonderful!" she said softly.

"So do you. Thank you for all your help," Alana said sincerely. Alex had lent a her gold evening bag, and the topaz and diamond earrings that swung like miniature chandeliers from her ears.

Alex inclined her head, her heavy raven hair drawn back into a classic chignon. "Kieran is home with your father?"

"He knew I'd be anxious," Alana explained.

"Of course." Alex touched her shoulder gently. "I just wanted to say hello, and tell you how lovely you look. I'd better get back to our guests now."

"Your mother is here." Alana looked towards the main table, arranged to seat twenty, where Sidonie Radcliffe in midnight-blue, looking light years younger than her age and sparkling with sapphires and diamonds, sat with her adored son, her Sydney friends, some VIP guests and the other three members of the committee besides Guy.

"She likes to come on these occasions," Alex murmured with a poignant smile. "Good luck now, Alana. You're the clear favourite—as you should be," she whispered, bending her head close to Alana's ear. "I'll see you later."

Alana wasn't the only one who kept their eyes on Alexandra Radcliffe as she walked back to the main table.

"Will you *quit* it, Rose?" Simon was saying, almost angrily, his face flushed.

"No, I mean it!" Rose replied earnestly.

"Mean what?" Alana intervened.

Rose fingered her pretty three-tiered earrings. "I was just telling Simon how handsome he looks. Anyone would think I was trying to proposition him."

"It's true, Simon," Alana chided him lightly. "You *do* look great." She turned her attention to their friends, Sally and Greg, asking if they had set their wedding date yet. Sally had already promised she and Rose they would be bridesmaids.

"Come on, now—you've been engaged six months," Rose said. 'Time to get married. Start a family. I can't wait to pick out my dress."

"To *help* pick out your dress," Sally said.

They were treated to a superb three-course dinner. Alana didn't feel hungry, although she had hardly eaten anything all day. A feeling painfully akin to dread seemed to be weighing her down.

"Laine, you're not eating anything," Simon murmured, looking at her with concern. "Try a mouthful of dessert. It's absolutely delicious!"

It certainly looked it. Luscious-looking strawberries had been arranged on a disc of crisp hazelnut shortbread, with a generous amount of champagne sabayon spooned over. A richly coloured strawberry coulis was spooned artfully around the plate, and there was a tiny sprig of fresh mint.

She picked up her spoon, intercepting a glaring look from Violette, who—surprise, surprise—hadn't managed to make it to the main table. She was seated a short distance away among her own crowd, and was wearing an electric-blue gown with a high straight neck, wasp-waisted. The severity of the top made much of the flounce of the full skirt that fell from her narrow hips. When she turned, most people gave a gasp. Almost the entire back was scooped out, revealing a good deal of smooth skin. A large sunburst brooch of diamonds, which Alana happened to know belonged to the girl's mother, was pinned to one side of the bodice. Alana thought she looked beautiful and very sophisticated. If only she could get that scowl off her face! Poor Violette. She hadn't yet discovered how to relax. If it were up to me, Alana thought, I would hand the prize to Violette. She wasn't trying to win anything. Violette *was*.

After the dessert had been served, serious table-hopping started as the dancing began. Rose and Sally had gone off together to the powder room, but Alana discreetly repaired her lipstick at the table, with Simon looking on with such reverence she might have been a religious icon.

"Okay?" she asked him, pouting a little. She couldn't figure out how to get through to Simon that although she loved him it wasn't and could never be a romantic love. It was much more sisterly. Her heart ached. The last thing she wanted to do was make Simon miserable, but she was going through a really difficult time now herself. Rose would have to do the nurturing for a while. Rose was so pretty she'd catch any man's attention.

Why, oh, why did people make the wrong choices?

"Perfect." Simon laughed, his eyes on her beautiful mouth. He positioned one of his hands over hers. "You look so wonderful I don't dare ask you to dance. I don't want to tread on your toes. I love your shoes. What do you call them?"

"Shoes. Or, if you want to get specific, slingbacks. If you don't want to dance, we can sit it out," Alana said, fully prepared to reject an over-enthusiastic admirer heading her way.

Simon glanced past her to smile. "Well, you can count your lucky stars. Guy is coming over. From the look of him, he seems set on changing your mind. I don't blame him. You two are really something to watch."

"Fred and Ginger!" Alana said, a little discordantly.

She glanced over her shoulder, watching Guy make his way towards them, looking as good as any man could or should. He was a real heartbreaker. She started to wonder if she had dreamed he had proposed marriage just a few days ago. If it wasn't a dream, what was she supposed to *say? I love you very, very much, Guy, but no.* She had always suffered from the sin of pride. He hadn't said a single word about loving *her.* Instead, he had come up with a serious proposal. An arrangement; a business deal. He was, after all, a high-profile businessman, a master of strategy. She had just about accepted he wanted her. Those kisses didn't lie. Did he count on falling in love with her eventually? Or had he seen too much of love destroying lives?

She had known Guy Radcliffe all her life. A decade ago she had hero-worshipped him. By the time she was sixteen it had morphed into an enormous adolescent crush. At around nineteen, to counteract the crush, she had taken to trying to take the mickey out of him. Now he had asked her to marry him. Not only that, he was waiting for a response from her. And she had to make it snappy.

She *had* dreamt it. It was possible to dream with one's eyes wide open.

The closer he got, the more her pulses throbbed. She might well faint by the time he arrived at their table. She could hear the adoring voices raised to greet him as he passed the tables. He would have a special smile for everyone. Guy was so charming he could sell ice-blocks to Eskimos.

"Marvellous evening, Guy!" Simon exclaimed in his familiar worshipful tones. "Everyone is having a great time."

"Seem to be," Guy responded warmly, one hand coming to rest on the curved rim of Alana's chair. "Alana, am I going to have to talk to your back?" he enquired with soft mockery.

"Of course not, Guy!" She turned slowly towards him.

Their eyes met. "You take my breath away," he said.

Simon's smile wavered uncertainly. Guy and Alana were looking at one another with a strange intensity. If he didn't know better, he'd say they appeared to be fascinated with one another. What could it mean? It wasn't simply friendly. It looked as if they had a secret understanding. That *couldn't* be the case…

Alana didn't answer, but she did let Guy take her hand as she rose.

Simon watched them move away as if he didn't exist. Was there something here he needed to worry about?

Softly, so softly it was almost inaudible, Rose tiptoed up behind Simon and whispered in his ear, "I can't help thinking Guy's got his eye on our Lana."

"*Guy* has?" Simon croaked.

"Well, yeah." Rose slipped into Alana's abandoned chair.

"No way!" Simon shook his head vigorously. "*I've* got feelings for Lainie." That settled it. Mother-dominated Simon might be but he had always managed to get pretty well everything he wanted.

"Well, of course you have," Rose soothed. "You've been friends since you were kids. But Lana's all grown-up now, Simon. She's following her heart."

"Her *heart?*" Simon repeated numbly. "You've got it wrong."

"You have to trust me." Rose sweetly patted his cheek. "Just look at them. Are they dancing or making love? Anyway, you can't sit here moping." She grabbed his hand. "Come with me. I'll teach you to tango!"

Simon wasn't the only one watching Guy and Alana as they moved with such spellbinding grace around the dance floor, Guy's dark head bent over Alana's, her long golden mane, centre-parted, curling sinuously around her face and down her back. The effect was quite magical.

Sidonie Radcliffe didn't see it that way. "What's going on *there?*" she demanded of her daughter, steering Alex to the cover of a handsome clump of golden canes in glazed pots.

"You disapprove?" A blind woman could see her mother wanted to break it up.

"Of course I disapprove." Sidonie made no effort to hide her dismay.

"I don't think Guy could make a better choice," Alex said, not terribly surprised at the turn of events.

"Well, you would, wouldn't you?" her mother replied sharply. "You've let her brother ruin your life. Beautiful as you are, I can see you still unmarried at forty." A ripple of malice passed across her striking face.

Alex had thought the same thing herself. Nevertheless, she managed wryly, "One isn't old and ugly at forty, Mother. You really hate them, don't you?" Did anything ever change?

"Why wouldn't I?" Sidonie sounded frighteningly bitter. "They're Annabel's children. Your father might have married me, but I was his second choice. Annabel was his great love."

"I'm sorry, Mama," Alex felt her mother's pain and lifelong resentment. "But he did love you, and he was faithful to you. Dad wasn't the sort of man who dishonoured his marriage vows. He wasn't the sort of man who would touch another man's wife."

Tears sparkled momentarily in Sidonie's eyes. "I don't need you to tell me that, thank you, Alexandra," she said tightly. "But we all know what kind of man Alan Callaghan is."

"A very sick man," Alex said. "I have an awful feeling he won't pull through this operation."

"Perhaps that's just as well," Sidonie muttered cruelly, her face pale beneath her impeccable make-up. "Roger won't wait for ever, Alex. He's devoted to you, but he wants you to make up your mind. So do I. You can't waste any more of your life on that seducer. I know he's got a powerful hold on you, but it's all sexual."

"It generally *is*," Alex commented wryly, her eyes following Alana's and Guy's slow, sensual progress.

"At least you've never let yourself fall pregnant to him again," Sidonie said, barely controlling the bitter resentment she still carried. Her best-laid plans—and she had had *such* plans for her beautiful teenage daughter—had been ruined. Alex, her perfect girl, had allowed herself to be seduced by an utterly unacceptable young man. Sidonie hated him. She had no more moved on than her daughter. But at least Keiran had stuck to the promise she had wrung from him. In Sidonie's view it was the only decent thing he had ever done.

Alex's face had that poignant look again. "You always blame Kieran, but it took the two of us, Mother. We mightn't have shown much wisdom in the timing, but we were mad for each other."

Sidonie's eyes flashed contempt. "I never thought you were *weak*, Alex," she said. "Why don't you try asking him if he'll marry you?" she challenged, with a chilling smile.

To Alex, it was like an actual slap in the face. She felt herself turn to a pillar of ice. What she saw in her mother's eyes caused her to gasp. "My God!"

Her mother stood motionless.

"What a fool I've been! What a *trusting* fool." The bubble had finally burst. The sound was like a crack of thunder.

Even the supremely self-confident Sidonie felt the vibrations. She suddenly became agitated, even though she knew agitation diminished control. "What? What is it?" she demanded, tugging on her spectacular necklace.

"I look at you, Mother, and I see a stranger," Alex said painfully. "I told Kieran the truth of what happened. I think you may have told him something different."

Sidonie's released breath was like the hiss of a snake. "Like what?" She spoke aggressively, but those glacial eyes of hers looked trapped.

Alex felt as though she was awakening from a nightmare. "Of *course!* Who would Kieran believe if not my mother?" she asked. "Oh, I bet you made it good. You can be very convincing when you want. It was *you* who invented the story of an abortion, knowing full well all the anguish that would bring. *You,* the mother I trusted with my life. And he believed you. Why not? You were Mrs David Radcliffe, a woman who would never stoop to sordid lies. I bet you swore him to secrecy as well? Told him to keep questioning me would only put me on the rack? God, Mother! What have you *done?*" Alex held up a hand as Sidonie went to speak. "No—please don't deny it. It's right there in your face."

Indeed it was, and with terrible clarity. Sidonie tried very hard to gather herself. "This is not the time or the place to have such a conversation, Alex," she said harshly. "Everything I've ever done has been in your best interests. All I'll say is this. The Callaghans, brother and sister, are a dangerous pair. Guy would be making a very serious mistake if he got involved with that girl. It would never work out—any more than your sick relationship with her brother has." She went to stalk off, her face tight, only Alex caught hold of her arm.

"Sick relationship?" she queried, keeping her voice very low. "I've heard you say that so many times. I've hated it, but I've tried to see where you as my mother are coming from. I trusted you absolutely. I was under the ridiculous impression you loved me."

"I do love you, Alex," Sidonie flashed back. "Even though you've made it hard. I repeat: everything I've done has been for you. Now, stop this right now—before people start to notice."

Gently Alex released her mother's arm. "Tonight has been a real eye-opener for me, Mother. A shaft of light has suddenly come into my life. You've kept your hateful secret a long time, but tonight, seeing Guy and Alana together, you were provoked into giving that secret away. Your plan to destroy my relationship with Kieran almost succeeded. We've wasted years—trying other relationships that could never go deep. Well, you'll have to forget Roger as a son-in-law. I've already told him his hopes are in vain. I love Kieran. I always will. The wicked part is you used any means at your disposal to drive us apart."

"There's nothing a mother wouldn't do to protect her child," Sidonie said, and gave a strange laugh that held no humour at all.

"Only, *Mother,* you have a heart of lead." There was infinite sadness in Alex's response.

No one would have dared to break in. Quite a few people were transfixed, watching Alana in Guy Radcliffe's arms. It wasn't just their expertise that was riveting the eye, their body language was even more revealing.

Violette's mother, Constance, moved in close to her daughter, giving her an ironic sideways look. "I can't imagine what he sees in her, can you? I mean, it can't be her looks!"

Violette rose from the table and dashed away.

On the area of the restaurant converted to a dance floor, even Alana felt defined as Guy's "woman". They hardly spoke. Neither of them was smiling. But Alana could feel herself falling deeper and deeper in love. What was happening to her was tremendous. She had often pictured herself dancing in Guy's arms, but she had found the reality physically breathtaking. She vaguely remembered all the other partners she had had over the years. She had gone along to all the dances. She had always been very much in demand. The difference between Guy and all those others was mind-blowing. It wasn't just his physical grace and sense of rhythm that was exceptional. She felt as if she was actually being made love to. If she lifted her head and he lowered his they could touch mouths. They were not kissing, but they might have been.

"I wish there was some place we could go." Guy looked down at her, his dark gaze intense. "I want to make love to you." So badly he was consumed by a primitive urgency. "I don't want to wait."

His words thrilled her so much Alana's eyelids fluttered closed. If his arms hadn't been encompassing her she thought she might even have fallen. She didn't want to wait either. She was ready. Waiting. Open. Desperate to be taken to his bed. She had made it her business to seek protection, so that she would be ready when he wanted her. There was such an inevitability about it.

They were standing still now. The music had stopped. Guy's warm hand brushed across the bare skin of her back. Her nipples were so hard she felt their peaks must be showing through the silk organza of her dress. What she felt for him was so overwhelming she was dizzied.

"Time to return to the world," Guy murmured wryly, as though he too was being wrenched from some deeply intimate secret place. "Oh, well—there's always tomorrow. And tomorrow. And tomorrow." He smiled at her ruefully, then escorted her back to her table.

Some twenty minutes later, the lights in the huge room were dimmed room and all voices stilled as Guy walked to the podium and held up his hand. A spotlight rained down on his dark head. He glanced at the card in his hand, then looked up to give the audience his marvellous smile, the flash of white teeth offset by the polished bronze of his skin. Guy Radcliffe was no ordinary man. He was Lord of the Valley.

"And now, ladies and gentlemen," he began, the special timbre of his voice working its magic, "it's my great pleasure to announce, on behalf of the committee, the winner of the title Most Beautiful Girl in Wangaree Valley."

He paused, a moment of drama, and the spotlight skipped

from him to the table where Alana was sitting with her friends. Three of the other young women there had entered the contest— Rose, Sally and Louise—all charming, and very attractive. Guy put out an arm. A fanfare went up, then a slow drumroll.

"And the winner is…" He spread it out, in time-honoured fashion. "Miss Alana Callaghan." His voice, had he known it, held tremendous satisfaction.

A few young women expelled disappointed sighs. One, the glamorous Violette Denby, actually turned up her nose— a gesture that didn't go down well with the guests seated around her.

"Alana would you come up to the dais, please?" Guy invited.

Simon helped Alana to her feet, the first one to kiss her cheek. "Congratulations, Lainie!" he said, bursting with pride. Genuinely thrilled for her, Rose, Sally and then Louise followed suit.

"When you go to the Napa Valley you're supposed to bring a friend," Rose prompted. "Keep me in mind!"

From around the large room there was so much clapping and cheering and loud whistles the noise almost raised the rafters.

"Go on, sweetie—you're on!" Rose gave Alana, who was standing rather shell-shocked, a little push. "Breathe in, breathe out!" she instructed.

People stood up as Alana made her way through the tables on her way to the dais. "*Bravo,* Alana. Well done!" Her mother's friend, Helen, embraced her warmly.

There was a bursting sensation in Alana's chest. She was that rare thing: a beautiful young woman who didn't dwell much on her looks.

When she moved past Violette's table she almost expected her cousin to poke out her tongue, but Violette confounded her by growling, "Congratulations!"

Alana kept her eyes trained on Guy's tall commanding figure as though he were her guiding star. Finally she reached him. He took her hand, staring down at her, then he carried it to his lips.

"Congratulations, Alana." He bent his head, his hair under the lights as shiny as a crow's wing, to kiss her cheek.

The audience loved it. Pretty well everyone rose to their feet, and as the volume of clapping increased the rest didn't dare remained seated. This was a great occasion for the Valley. The harvest was over. It would be a vintage year.

A gold diadem of exquisitely wrought gold vine leaves with a gold medallion at its centre, studded with a cluster of glittering garnets to represent the fruit of the vine, was held high by Guy. The crowd went quiet as he placed it gently on Alana's head, finding exactly the position that suited her best.

There were little cries and gasps of admiration and delight. Another boom of applause. Alana appeared so bright and beautiful—so much like her mother. A few wounds around the room opened up, then miraculously closed.

She walked a little way, so everyone could see her.

The clapping got harder. There couldn't have been a more popular choice. Then the cheering and laughter broke into, "Speech, *speech!*"

Alana moved back to Guy, "I don't have a speech prepared," she whispered in a worried voice.

He leaned towards her. "Just say what you're thinking right at this moment."

Her speech was short, but it turned out to be brilliant. It was funny. It was touching. It started out and finished with thoughts of her mother.

When she was finished, many people in the room who had known Annabel Callaghan, born Denby, discreetly blew their noses. Charles Denby, extraordinarily enough, was one of them. Things had to change from this point on, he thought.

* * *

Her father was asleep when she finally arrived home. She looked in on him, then closed the door gently, going back to the living room, where Kieran was waiting for her. They talked about the function, and Kieran was full of brotherly pride in her win.

"Uncle Charles actually came over to offer me his congratulations."

"Good grief. I wonder what it cost the old man to do an about-face?" Kieran laughed. "How did Alex look?" He turned away, seemingly casual, to switch off lights.

"So, so beautiful." Alana sighed. "A beautiful, tragic woman, like the heroine in an opera. You know—the one bewailing the loss of her lover? It's there in those great dark eyes. She wore a superb white gown with pearls. Anyway you'll be able to see all the photographs. What time did Dad turn in?"

"Not long after your call. That was the big excitement of his night. We watched the football earlier. I asked Buddy over. He's a good kid. He broke into a dance when I told him you'd won. Dad wept tears of joy. He's much more at peace with himself these days."

"Isn't he? Thank goodness!" Alana murmured fervently.

Around eight o'clock the next morning—she'd had a rare sleep-in—Alana took a tray into her father's room. On it was freshly squeezed orange juice, a slice of papaya, two soft-boiled eggs, wholegrain toast, and a little pot of Vegemite to go with it.

She was about to call *wakey, wakey,* when she realised with a shock her father wasn't in his bed. She knew he wasn't in the bathroom. The door was open. There was no sound. So where had he spent the night? Her heart began an ominous thud. Still carrying the tray she retraced her steps, pausing outside the master bedroom. The door was very slightly ajar. She used the edge of the silver tray to push it open.

Her father lay on his back, his hands folded across his

chest, his eyes shut, his face serene. He hadn't turned back the quilt. He lay on top of it. It was one of her mother's beautiful patchwork quilts—a work of art.

Her heart felt as if it was being entombed in ice. Her limbs went numb. She was frozen in position, yet she called with quiet anguish, "Dad?"

No response. But then she hadn't expected one, had she? A great winged being had come for her father; one that had caused him no fear.

She thought she might have cried out her brother's name. Kieran should be here with her now. The silver tray started to wobble dangerously. Soon it and its contents would crash to the floor. But that was nothing. She didn't care.

"Lana?"

Through a fog, she heard Kieran's voice. He had returned home.

Kieran was to tell her later he had felt such a chill, even in the bright sunshine, he had returned to the homestead without completing his chores. Now he moved swiftly along the passageway, his every movement urgent. He took the tray out of his sister's shaking hands and set it down on a hall table.

"Dad won't wake up," she told him, sounding to his ears as she'd used to as a little girl.

He could see she was already going into shock. Alana had had to endure so much. He threw his arms around her and she clung to him desperately.

"Dad will never be unhappy again, Lana," he tried to console her. "His life was over when Mum died."

Her heart broke.

CHAPTER NINE

THE day of the funeral was one of stifling heat, although everyone in the Valley had thought the worst of the high temperatures was over. Father Brennan, the village priest, presided at the Mass, and later at the graveside. It seemed as if everyone in the Valley had turned out, filling the church and spilling out into the grounds where the golden wattles were at the height of their beauty.

As though it was perfectly reasonable, and there had been no estrangement whatever, the Denbys were in attendance. Charles Denby, in fact had shepherded his family to the pew directly behind Alana and Kieran, murmuring condolences to them as he passed. They even sounded sincere.

"God!" breathed Kieran to his sister, not one to forgive and forget.

When the time came Guy spoke movingly—emotionally in control, but with such a sensitive, comforting intonation.

I could have fallen in love with your voice alone, Alana thought, biting down hard on her lip. Many tears had fallen in private. For the service she had decided to be strong.

Others came forward. Alana knew her mother's friend, Helen, was to speak. Helen had offered. Simon, who sat beside her, held her hand.

If Alana isn't going to fall in *love with me, at least she will* always *love* me, Simon thought, feeling some small degree of consolation. We're *pals*. Alan Callaghan's death had brought about a few radical changes, though the night of The Naming had turned Simon's thoughts around. He would take another look at Rose...

At one point in the graveside service Kieran Callaghan distracted everyone's attention by suddenly throwing out an arm and clasping Alex Radcliffe to him as though they couldn't be apart. Alex Radcliffe further distracted the mourners by adhering tenderly to his side. There was no real explanation for why she had been standing right next to him, other than the fact her brother Guy and their cousin Simon were flanking Alana. No one had a clue Kieran Callaghan and Alex Radcliffe were still such good friends. Or more accurately, so close.

"Well, we needn't wonder who Kieran's woman of mystery is any more," Guy murmured to Alana as he led her away to his car. "It's Alex."

Even in the midst of her grief Alana hadn't been slow to pick up on that. Of *course* it was. How could she have been so stupid? In one staggering moment of revelation Keiran and Alex had shown themselves to be powerfully involved. They had even walked off together, Kieran's arm around Alex's slender shoulders as though he couldn't bear to let her go.

Somehow Alana got through the wake. Yet again Guy had come to the rescue, organizing the food and drink which seemed to be expected on even the most mournful occasions. Alana couldn't for the life of her work out why. Couldn't people function without cramming down food? Still, the people who packed into Briar Ridge's homestead were for the most part good, caring people she and Kieran had known all their lives.

Simon's mother, Rebecca, had even stunned the throng by showing she had a smile. Pale-faced, she had taken Alana's hand, telling her if she ever needed someone to talk to she was "just up the road". In the space of a few days Rebecca had turned from an enemy to a friend. A phenomenon that was unique—although Guy's strengthening presence in Alana's life *would* have appeared to her as taking the heat off her son.

A further shock was in store when Charles Denby offered to lend his niece and nephew money to "keep the farm going."

"I haven't done enough for you, Alana," he told her heavily, as though he felt the guilt. "I adored your mother, my only sister. You're *so* like her."

"Adored her, did he?" said Kieran wrathfully, his blue eyes burning. He was about to continue in that vein, only Alana looked so utterly spent he kept the rest of what he was going to say to himself.

Finally the last of the mourners, who happened to be Uncle Charles and his family—now apparently *their* family—left.

"Hypocrites, the lot of them!" Kieran said, the expression on his handsome face an indicator that he had endured more than enough.

Only Guy and Alex remained, sitting quietly in the living room, behind the scenes.

"I'm taking Alana back to the house with me, Kieran," Guy said. "You're very welcome to come too." Although he meant it, Guy had a very good idea Kieran would stick with Alex, who had to make the return trip to Sydney for a big art showing the following night.

Alex confirmed it. "Kieran's coming back to Sydney with me," she explained quietly. "I know it's a sad time, but a big international art dealer is in town for only a very short while. I'd like Kieran to meet him and perhaps show him some of his work."

"What? Bring the dealer back here?" Alana asked in surprise.

Alex's magnolia skin flushed. "*I* have some excellent examples of Kieran's work at my apartment, Alana."

"Oh!" How had she never seen what had been happening? It hadn't been right under her nose, but still...

"Well, well, well!" said Guy, as Alex and Keiran drove away.

"There was always a flock of girls after Kieran," Alana said. "I used to wonder why he never settled on any of them for long."

"The same with Alex and the boys. The truly extraordinary thing is given the way they feel, why haven't they *done* something about it?" Guy asked. "You saw what they're like when they don't bother to put up the usual front. They're long-term *lovers!*"

Alana looked at him with shadowed hazel eyes, wondering how she would have got through these days of trauma without his presence and splendid support. "Alex has always seemed to me as though she has some tragic secret. Could I be wrong about that?"

"Like what?" Guy asked, his black brows knitting. He sat down beside her and took her hand in his.

"How should I know? You're her brother." She was close to tears.

He drew her head onto his shoulder, feeling a torrent of emotion himself. "All I can tell you is I'm pretty sure Kieran was Alex's first love. When they were teenagers they were inseparable—don't you remember?"

"When they split up, and Alex went off to Sydney, I thought Kieran had decided she was way out of his league."

"Whatever that league may be?" Guy murmured in a wry voice. "Do you think I'm way out of *your* league?" He looked down on her, utterly vulnerable, utterly his object of desire.

"I thought you wanted to make do with me," she responded.

Guy stood up, gently drawing her with him. "You're exhausted. I'm taking you home."

* * *

They fled the Valley chased by grief. Kieran drove Alex's powerful car faster than he should, as if it gave him the best chance of losing whatever was in pursuit. She didn't have to glance at his sculpted face, illuminated by the glow from the dashboard, to recognise the pain and sorrow that consumed him. They were approaching the outskirts of the city before he slowed down. She breathed a sigh of relief. The last thing she wanted was to catch sight of a police car on their tail. Kieran was an excellent driver, but rules were rules. Still, he manoeuvred through the traffic, changing lanes until they drove into the underground car park of her apartment block in record time.

Inside the apartment Kieran threw off his jacket, trying to get hold of himself. He felt like crashing on to the bed with Alex—his beautiful Alex—locked in his arms. Whatever had happened to them in the past, it suddenly didn't matter now. If he lost Alex he would be the loneliest man on earth. He loved her. He always would. She was his only chance at happiness. Hadn't his poor father been a one-woman man?

"God, I'm a mess," he said aloud. "One big emotional mess. But I swear I'm going to get myself together." He thrust a hand through his thick blond hair, dragging it back from his broad forehead. He was deeply conscious of his change of attitude. Something almost supernatural was giving him a second chance.

"Why wouldn't you be?" Alex comforted him quietly, removing her black jacket to expose a delicately ruffled white chiffon blouse. "It was a simply terrible day."

"I'm sure I couldn't have got through it without you," Kieran said, moving to the drinks cabinet. "The same goes for Lana and Guy. I always knew Guy mattered to her, however much she tried to hide it, but she *loves* him!"

"Aren't you happy about that?" Alex searched his burning blue eyes, herself very pale.

"Oh, yes!" Kieran exclaimed in surprise. "You don't think

I'd leave my sister with just anyone? Guy is the best bloke in the world. *I'm* the bad guy who is so self-righteous! What would you like to drink?" He turned. God, she was beautiful! Her beauty broke his heart. He had been working on a portrait of her. He had to have it finished by her birthday. A big surprise! He hadn't thought he would be any good at portraiture, but he was happy with what he had done so far. Even to his highly critical eye it was good.

"Don't worry about me." Alex shook her hair free so it cascaded around her face and down her back. "I think I'll have a shower to unravel."

"Neither of us have had anything to eat," Kieran commented, his glance tender. "It was impossible to think of eating at the house. Would you like me to order something in?"

Tears were standing in the corners of Alex's dark eyes. She turned away, raising a furtive finger to wipe them away. There was something different about Kieran. It was as though they were drawing closer now, rather than moving apart. Was it possible he was close to forgiving her? Forgiving her for something she had never done?

"I've got plenty of eggs and smoked salmon, if that would do?" she called, beginning to move down the corridor. She was exhausted—not only from the funeral, that had filled her with sadness, but from her own concerns. Plus, there would be a lot of running around to do for the following night's art showing.

Kieran sigh was deep in his throat. "Fine," he called back, swallowing a mouthful of bourbon neat. "Don't be long. I can't bear you out of my sight."

Warm water cascaded all over Alex's face and body. It went a way towards restoring her calm. She tried to think of the right way to tell Kieran the truth. Her mother had *lied.*

As with all lies, there had been a reason. She knew her mother well. Her mother loved her. She had been shocked out of her mind when she'd gone to her to confess she had carried

Kieran's child for almost three months. And in the space of a few minutes she had lost it. She knew her mother had had so many dreams centred on her. She had destroyed them by getting pregnant so young, without even finishing her studies. Her mother had decided there and then to wipe Kieran out of her life. And she had chosen what she had considered the most effective way to do that. She had made Kieran believe the girl he loved and trusted totally had given him no say whatsoever in what happened to their unborn child. She had given him no chance to try to talk her out of an abortion that had never happened. She had made her decision without him. It was her life, her body. She was too young for such responsibility. There were profound consequences to reckless behaviour. It happened in life.

True to his promise, Kieran had laboured for years to say *nothing*. He had stuck grimly to his promise not to betray her mother's confidence. Only her mother's lie had left a huge standing obstacle in their lives. Kieran, so volatile on the surface, was underneath a deeply sensitive man.

She had her head tilted back, letting the water run over her face and down over her breasts, when he entered the bathroom.

"Come out of there," he said thickly, already rock hard at the sight of her. Her slender arms were raised to her temples in a motion that lifted her chest. Her long raven hair was knotted and pulled back tightly from her face. She looked as though she had been out naked in the rain. Beads and rivulets of water glistened all over the curves and planes of her body, her satin smooth buttocks, that little silky triangle of intimate hair. He picked up a bathtowel as she turned off the tap. "Come on out to me." He walked to the shower door, opening it for her.

His tone of voice told her he wanted her. Right then. Kieran was a very sexual man.

"I'll dry you."

She stepped onto the bathmat with a leap of the heart. He used the soft towel on her as well as his mouth, slowly covering every inch of her body, the little swells and dells, the insides of her thighs and legs, her intimate flesh, sliding to his knees to do so.

"Kieran!" she whispered, enveloped in an indescribable heat. She moved her hands down in a near frenzy, to lift his golden head. Saw his eyes. He let the towel fall to the tiles, then he rose to his commanding height, opening the petals of her soft, moist lips as he held her crushed against his demanding body.

"I could never be separated from you for long." A sound like a low growl issued from his throat.

He stood kissing and caressing her, but the time came when he could no longer contain himself. He lifted her into his arms, exulting in her exquisite womanliness. It fell all around them like a silken enveloping cloak.

At Wangaree's splendid homestead, Alana was sitting in the dream of a kitchen, watching Guy, CEO of Radcliffe Enterprises, move about it as though preparing a meal was child's play. Wangaree might be his castle, but he had taken it upon himself to make them both a Thai stir-fry chicken dish that was to be served with jasmine rice.

"Where's Gwen?" she asked, too worn out to take her elbows off the table. Gwen was the housekeeper. She had worked for the Radcliffes for over forty years.

"I said it was okay if she spent a few days with her daughter."

"It's pretty funny, your doing the cooking," she remarked wryly.

"Sometimes I surprise myself." He gave her a half smile. "When you try it, you'll find it's good."

"It smells good. Chilli, coriander, ginger… I'm sorry I can't help you."

"I don't want you to help me. I want you to just sit there

and do nothing. Why not drink that glass of wine? It might help relax you."

"I don't feel like a normal person," she said sadly, taking not a sip but a gulp.

"You'll feel a little bit better after you've had something to eat," Guy commented. He was trying hard to comfort her, while understanding there was precious little comfort to be offered on such a day. There would be a great deal of mourning over this bereavement. The situation was just too painful.

A few minutes later Guy put a beautiful blue and white bowl in front of her. It contained a steaming mound of jasmine rice with the fragrant stir-fry ladled over it.

"Thank you." She looked up at him gravely. "You're being awfully kind to me."

"You're awfully easy to be kind to." He was afraid of saying any more. Now wasn't the time to burden her with his overload of emotion. Instead he resorted to an encouraging briskness. "Okay, then—off you go!"

She rewarded him with a laugh. "You should ring a bell."

She took hold of her fork. Because he had gone to so much trouble, she made a real effort to eat.

"It *is* good," she said, after a minute, finding him watching her as if she was a difficult-to-please child.

"Thank you. Thank you very much, Ms Callaghan. I don't know that I like the note of surprise, though." He sat down opposite her.

"Oh, come on—you know I'm joking." Her smile wobbled. She gave a shuddering sigh.

"Don't cry," he said. *"Please."* He remembered how she had once said she would never cry in front of him. But then she had not been expecting this further tragedy. He knew if those tears started rolling he'd lose it and pull her into his arms. "No need to talk. Just finish your dinner."

"You're a wonderful man," she said. "You sound like you might feed me like a baby."

"Take it seriously," he warned. "I just might do that, before you droop into sleep. By the way, I got hold of some sleeping tablets for you—just in case you feel like taking one."

"So I can fall into oblivion, you mean?" Her beautiful eyes met his. "I'm not a weak woman, am I, Guy?"

It took every last bit of his self-control not to move around the table and gather her up. He wanted to carry her upstairs. Show her in every way he knew, how much she meant to him. But it seemed like sacrilege to have these primeval urges when she was so supremely vulnerable.

"Of course you aren't," he said, his tone a little harsh, from the strength of his feelings. "You're really brave. Uncommonly brave. Now take another mouthful."

"Yes, Sir Guy!" She gave a plangent laugh. "I won't have one of the sleeping pills, thank you. I don't like taking things unless I absolutely have to."

"Well, we'll see," he said, and left it at that.

Alana moved out of her bedroom into the spacious hallway of the upper level. It was more like an art gallery, with its fine paintings, valuable antiques on carved stands, and its chairs set at intervals. She stood looking around her for a minute or two, trying to get her bearings. It was such a big house—a true mansion. She had thought as a child she could easily get lost in it. She could get lost in it now.

It seemed hard to believe, but she had fallen asleep the moment her head hit the pillow. Had Guy given her a sleeping draught after all? He had made her a glass of warm milk accompanied by a shortbread biscuit at around ten o'clock, after which he had walked her upstairs to the luxurious bedroom that had been made up for her. It was Alex's bedroom. Her mother had had it redecorated to encourage Alex to come home more often. It had a very "French" feel to it, Sidonie Radcliffe being a self-confessed Francophile. Now *she* was occupying the room specially prepared for Alex.

Sidonie Radcliffe didn't like her. It was easy to understand why. Sidonie most probably had strong feelings about the role her own mother, Annabel, had played in the Radcliffe marriage. Yet surely her own parents had been happy? Hadn't they? They had hardly ever argued. When they walked about Briar's Ridge they had walked hand in hand. Her mother had laughed at all her father's jokes, especially the Irish ones. Alana *had* to believe they'd loved one another. Her mother had been the very centre of her father's life.

Guy had left the hall sconces on. That would be for her benefit, of course. It was obvious he hadn't wanted her to feel lost in a strange house. Even the corridor seemed very, very long.

What was she doing out here in her nightgown? Suddenly she felt seriously befuddled. She turned about, taking a few halting steps back into her room. She wasn't like this normally. She wasn't prone to confusion. But from the moment she had come awake in the semi-dark she'd realised she hated to be on her own. Kieran had his Alex. She had a powerful urge to be with Guy. She wanted the wonderful comfort of his arms around her. He had offered her marriage, hadn't he? He shouldn't be surprised, then, if she went to him.

The main problem was she didn't know where he was. She turned around and then walked on uncertainly. The bedrooms to either side were empty. She knew there were twelve bedrooms in the mansion. She wasn't sure if Guy had told her which one was his. If he had, she couldn't recall which.

God, she felt dreadful—weaker than she had ever felt in her life. She came to a halt, then called out tentatively, "Guy?"

There was absolute silence. She felt a complete fool. He

would be fast asleep—though she wasn't at all sure what time it was. What was she supposed to do? Walk up and down for the rest of the night, crying out his name?

Please, Guy, where are you? I need you.

She knew she was acting oddly. However, she had some excuse. She was in an intensely emotional state.

"Alana?" It was a voice she would know if she heard it anywhere.

Thank goodness!

"What are you doing there, wandering about? Are you okay?" He had come by way of the staircase, which meant he had been downstairs. Now he was moving swiftly towards her, the embodiment of the protective male.

"No, I'm not!" She shook her head. "Were you sleeping downstairs?" The curious thing was he looked virtually the same as when he had shown her to her room hours earlier. He hadn't gone to bed at all.

"I had a bit of a problem sleeping," he admitted. "Actually I was reading."

"Gosh, it must be a good book. You'll have to lend it to me." She stared up at him with over-wrought eyes. "What time is it?" She wasn't aware she was whispering.

"Not all that late," he said. "Two o'clock. Do you want a little company?" He said it in his usual fashion, though he knew he could be putting himself in a situation that would require all his will-power.

"Oh, yes, *please*," she said gratefully, turning to retreat to her room.

"I'll stay until you fall asleep again," he told her gently. "I did suggest a sleeping pill."

"You should have taken one yourself."

"Then I wouldn't have heard your voice."

"I need you, Guy," she said.

It sounded more aggrieved than desirous. "Good. I like to

be needed." They were inside the room now, sumptuous by any standards.

"Take off your robe and hop into bed," he said. "I'll spread out on the chaise."

His voice, the voice that fascinated her, was absolutely gentle, yet his face looked tense. She was beginning to think she had made a big mistake. Did he *really* want to be here with her? Was that what was bothering him? Maybe he wanted to finish that great book?

She slid the silk robe off her shoulders, then stood beside the bed in her nightdress. It was a virginal white, pure cotton, with pintucks and little pearl buttons, and bouquets of pink roses in blue baskets embroidered here and there.

It wasn't a seductive or glamorous garment, Guy thought. Nothing like his sister's exquisite lingerie. But she was pretty and *so* innocent, with her long flowing hair a glittering gold in the light from the bedside lamp. Guy felt a great rush of protectiveness at war with the white heat in his loins.

He took a step towards the bed. "Come on, now. I'll tuck you in." It was amazing how normal his voice sounded when he was having to deal with an aching hunger.

"Please don't talk to me like I'm a child," she said.

"Poor little one!"

She was in the bed and he was looking down at her. Her beautiful hazel eyes were swimming with tears. She put out a hand to touch his. "I don't want you over there on the chaise, Guy. I want you *here*."

It took everything he had in him to clamp down on his desire. He spoke carefully. "Alana, I can't lie beside you and not want to make love to you. You surely must know that?"

She looked up into his taut face. "I'm not in the least sure. You've been treating me like a favourite cousin all evening, when I thought you were thinking about marrying me?"

His brilliant eyes flared. "Not *thinking* I want to marry you, Alana. I *am* going to marry you—in as short a time as is decent."

"You think I'll grow on you?" she asked ironically.

"Don't be silly." If he kissed her now he'd be lost. He began to move away.

"Unless you lie beside me I *won't* marry you," she called, as though issuing an ultimatum. "Are you going to do it?"

She felt so strange! Sad, disoriented, yet madly excited too. She wanted to feel the full length of his body beside her. She wanted to move right up against him. He didn't even have to touch her for her whole body to tremble.

"Okay," he said crisply, as though coming to a sudden decision. "Move over."

She did so immediately, her expression indicating she had won a victory. "Aren't you going to feel uncomfortable in your clothes?"

He couldn't help it. He groaned. "Alana, I have no intention of removing them until you're in a stronger frame of mind. I have, however, removed my shoes."

He lowered his long lean frame onto the bed beside her, taking care to lie on top of the bedclothes while she was under them. With a grunt he settled a couple of pillows behind his head, then dared to look down at her. She was turned on her side towards him. He could see the upward swell of her breasts, delicate as roses. One arm reached across him.

"Now go to sleep," he admonished.

She sighed. "If you add *like a good girl,* I'll scream."

"I might join you," he told her tersely.

A moment's silence, then, "*Hold* me."

I can't do this, he thought, his heart and senses and mind desperate to give in to the driving, shocking urge to take her. She was there to be taken. His living desire. Only how could he when she was in this state of enormous distress? That alone made him draw back. He wanted her to know exactly what she was doing when they came together. But she was making it impossibly hard. He wasn't a saint. His thoughts weren't saintly in the least. He was a man who urgently wanted the beautiful young woman lying so trustingly beside him. He wanted the exquisite pleasure of a mating with her beautiful virgin body. Who would have dreamt she had kept herself for him?

When she spoke, her voice was soft and sad. "I'm sorry. I didn't mean to embarrass you. I know it isn't the time." Not for intimacy.

Her eyelids shut to close him out, and slowly, carefully, he drew her body towards him, so her honey-gold head was lying against his shoulder.

"Dad has gone and left us," she murmured, snuggling in closer in an acute need for comfort. "I'm going to miss him terribly."

Guy's expression was infinitely tender. "Of course you are. I'll miss him too." He began to stroke her hair very gently, wanting so much to make her a part of himself but, beyond that, wanting what was best for *her*.

Finally, as he continued to soothe her, she slid into sleep.

Just as at home, a lone kookaburra signalled the dawn. Alana whirled up from sleep, her mouth opening in a gasp as she realised where she was. She vividly remembered Guy's stroking her hair with exquisite gentleness the night before. Nothing after that. He wasn't in the room, but a featherlight rug bordered in satin lay in a heap on the chaise. Obviously he had spent some part of the night there. Her memories were all tangled up. Hadn't she invited him into her bed? On the very night her father had been laid to rest? She pressed a hand against her heart, feeling it break. Both Guy and her father must be deeply ashamed of her—as she now was of herself. What had got into her? She flinched away from her advances, and from Guy's rejection. She wasn't the object of his desire. She was the young woman he had chosen for his own reasons to marry.

She felt gutted.

Four minutes later she had put on the clothing she had brought with her—jeans and a white tank top—and pulled a pair of flatties on her feet. She would pick up the rest of her things later. She was going home. She had made a fool of herself, even if the aftermath of the funeral was a hazy blur. The pain was awful. She could have been forgiven for clinging to him like a drowning woman in a stormy sea, but not for trying to seduce him. That now seemed to her profane. She was pathetic and ridiculous.

She made it out of the house via the verandah, then down the rear stairs. No one was about.

Horses were in the home paddock. She whistled one up, throwing herself up on its bare back.

"Come on, boy!" She clutched the gelding's mane, thumped its sides with her heels. A born horsewoman, she didn't hesitate for a minute to ride bareback. Briar's Ridge was barely a mile away.

She had only been home a few minutes when the phone rang. She made no move to answer it. It wouldn't be Kieran. Not at this hour. He had rung from Sydney the previous night. Besides, she was supposed to be with Guy. She let the phone ring out. She had to get a grip on herself. But how? she wondered. Nothing about her seemed to be functioning properly—her heart, her mind, even her legs. She walked into the kitchen to make herself a cup of tea and maybe a slice of toast. It was a terrible thing to lose all good sense. But that was what falling in love had done to her. For the first time in her life she felt inadequate in her own eyes.

The kettle had scarcely boiled before she heard a car pull

into the drive. She stood rooted to the spot, recognising the sound of the engine. She couldn't hide. She had to go to the door. She had no other option. She had actually stolen one of his horses.

Guy came up the short flight of steps, a faint pallor beneath his tanned skin. "Well, at least you're okay," he said tensely. "What the hell did you think you were doing? One of the boys saw you riding hell for leather bareback across the Valley."

"No harm to the horse," she said, tossing her head. "Is that what you've come to check on? Your horse?"

Guy frowned darkly. "Why are you like this?"

"Why are you like *you?*" she hurled back at him, almost running back inside the house. Anything to get away from him.

He literally zoomed after her, spinning her around against him. "Alana, what is it? Tell me and we can sort it out."

"I'm telling you nothing," she gritted, loving him so much she hated him too. It was a grim feeling. "But I do have to thank you, Guy—for everything you've done for us. So thank you." She might as well have added, *and good riddance.* "You've been wonderful—as befitting Guy Radcliffe, Lord of the Valley—but—"

"Shut up!" His hands tightened on her. He was outraged. All the ardour he felt for her, held repressed for so long, was suddenly, fatally, violently ignited. Every man had his limits. He had reached his. To add to his outrage, he had stayed awake the entire night, battling the punishing desire to go to her, take her for himself. What a reward! She had insulted his integrity. He had *not* succumbed to his elemental passion, yet she was looking at him as if he had brutally ravished her, stripped her of that virginal little nightdress and taken his fill of her, mindless of her cries.

It was not to be tolerated.

"Guy!"

A rising panic was in her voice. She had never seen this dark side of him.

"I'm not going to hurt you, you little fool!" His black eyes flashed. "Look at me."

Her heart was knocking fiercely against her ribs. "You're holding me so tight I can't run away and hide."

"Nor are you going to. I love you. I would never hurt you," he said furiously. "Why are you shivering and shaking?"

"It's the way you're holding me," she moaned, past all pretence.

Immediately he gentled his grip. "I'm sorry."

"Don't be. I *want* you to hold me. But with love. I'm desperate for you to love me. I thought…last night…I thought…"

"Tell me?" His hand slid to her satiny throat, half enclosing it with his long fingers.

"It must have seemed to you I was trying to seduce you into my bed. I'm sorry. I'm so ashamed. My only excuse is I was so dreadfully lonely. The house is so big, and it felt like you were a couple of blocks away. I couldn't seem to stop myself."

For a few moments he looked at her with a tense, questioning stare. "Then you'll understand if I can't stop myself either." His strong hands slid down her body to grasp her hips. He pulled her in to him, leaving her in no doubt of his arousal.

But there was something she desperately needed to say. "I love you," she exclaimed ardently, as if he mightn't quite believe her. "I think I've *always* loved you. You're someone I can love and honour. Someone I want to—"

His mouth covered hers so completely she couldn't get to finish. *Someone I want to share my life with.* He seemed to know all the same. All she had to do was hold on to him and never let go.

At some stage kissing wasn't enough. He picked her up,

carrying her up the stairs with little effort. She stretched out on her bed.

"Do we need protection?" he asked, his voice urgent.

She shook her head. "It's perfectly okay."

For a moment he stayed where he was, sitting on the side of the bed, saying nothing. He stared down at her as she lay, her eyes huge, her breasts rising and falling, her beautiful hair fanning out over the bed cushions.

"There's nothing I wouldn't do for you, Alana," he said. "I wanted you desperately last night, but I felt I would be taking advantage of a very sad situation. Never think for a second I was rejecting you. I was electric for you—as I am now. Tell me. You want this, don't you?"

How could he doubt it? Her expression was one of immense longing. "I want nothing more in the world," she said.

He swooped then to kiss her deeply, ardently, his hand moving to her shoulders, pushing the straps of her tank top and bra down her arms.

It was the beginning of an ecstasy that was to mount and mount, turning her into a creature of pure sensation. He removed her clothes, very slowly, very gently, all the while studying her, his dark eyes deeply desirous, and when he was finished he stood up and began to strip off his own clothing.

Excitement poured into her, flooding every artery. Her heart beat and flapped wing-like in her ears. Finally he was with her, the splendid male, spreading her arms wide as his mouth went down on her breast…

"I'll go slowly," he murmured tenderly. "Just say what you want, what you don't want, what you're comfortable with, what you're not. I want this to be the most marvellous experience for you. One we'll remember all our lives." The voice she loved vibrated with something akin to wonder. "I can't begin to explain it, my beautiful Alana, but I feel like this is the very first time for me too."

* * *

That evening Sidonie Radcliffe made a late entrance to the art showing, along with a select party of friends. As expected the gallery was crowded. As expected, red stickers were all over the paintings—thirty in all, displayed to perfection in two interlocking rooms. Morris Templeton was a long-established artist with a cult following. Sidonie had a few of his paintings in her own apartment, all increasing handsomely in value. Across the room she saw Alex, looking absolutely wonderful. She was so proud of her beautiful, clever daughter, talking to the artist himself. Like all men, Templeton, a known womaniser, looked fascinated.

A few moments later she caught sight of Keiran Callaghan as he moved with Colin Scholes, an art critic, into the main room. He stood head and shoulders over poor Colin, making him look like a rotund puppet. She had to hand it to her daughter's lover—he was a very glamorous looking young man. That leonine shock of blond hair—too long, of course—suited him. No one looking at him in his designer suit, black with a black shirt and no tie, would believe he was a humble sheep farmer. He looked like a film star.

Well, she had come here with a job to do. She had to do it. Like it or not. She didn't lack guts. She had done everything in her power to split the two of them up, but in the end it hadn't worked out. She had put the well-documented "aversion therapy" to the test, but although it had worked on him to a degree, it hadn't proved powerful enough to keep them from re-finding each other. Her beautiful daughter and Annabel Callaghan's son were bound together. She had to accept it or lose her daughter altogether. It was terrible what a parent was expected to do. But hadn't the whole business over the years begun to weigh increasingly heavily on her conscience? Everything had spun out of her control. When it came down to it, life itself was out of anyone's control. That was the terror if it.

The very last thing she had ever anticipated as all four were growing up—Guy and Alana, Kieran and Alex—was that they would fall in love with each other. She had seen her adored son with Alana, the mirror image of her mother. He *loved* her. Oh the irony! Moreover, Guy would marry her. She fully expected it would happen, after a period of mourning for the father. Like Charles Denby, Sidonie had decided she had to make a complete about-face. If she didn't she would not be able to retain the love and respect of her son and daughter. The prospect was unthinkable. Besides, she would make a marvellous grandmother.

Sidonie saw that Kieran was for the moment free. She had to move fast. A man who looked like that generally got mobbed. Swiftly she forged a path towards him. A beautiful, powerful, mature woman, the source of ongoing strife and pain, was ready to eat the humblest of humble pies. The really strange thing was, it brought with it an unexpected sense of freedom.

Confession really was good for the soul!

EPILOGUE

Four months later

THE wedding of Guy Radcliffe and Alana Callaghan took place at the bridegroom's splendid, sprawling country estate, historic Wangaree Station. The actual ceremony was held in its charming old private chapel, built in the Gothic revival style in the late 1880s for the Radcliffe family and their servants. It hadn't been in use as a place of worship since the late 1940s, when the two Radcliffe sons and the men of the Valley who had survived had returned home from World War II, but it had been splendidly maintained.

Guy's mother and father had been married in a Sydney cathedral, to much pomp and glory, but Guy and Alana had wanted their wedding to be a country affair. This was their way of showing their love for each other and for the Valley. The Valley in turn was thrilled by their decision.

Family and close friends had the privilege of attending the wedding ritual. They packed the chapel, lavishly decorated for the occasion with a veritable Eden of cream and white flowers, and with huge satin bows tied to the end of the polished cedar pews. The chapel, though small, was really very handsome, standing in its own grounds, with beautiful surrounding rose gardens that had been brought to the peak of perfection for the big day. Other guests, close to three hundred, had been invited to the reception, which was held in the magnificent grounds, which now looked more like the Botanic Gardens, under vast cream and gold marquees which appeared magical, floating on top of the lush green lawns.

The beautiful bride—none could eclipse her—wore a ravishing gown in the grand romantic fashion. Everyone said it was glorious, and it suited her to perfection. The bodice was strapless, encrusted with sparking crystals and seed pearls and with a tiny handspan waist, and the skirt was wonderfully billowing. The bride had elected to have an extravagantly full veil to shimmer around her and follow her in a train as she walked down the aisle on the arm of her stunningly handsome brother, Kieran. The Valley had recently learned that Keiran was making a mark in, of all places, the *art* world. Everyone suspected Alexandra Radcliffe had a lot to do with that…

The bridal veil was held in place by an amazing headdress, featuring at its centre a large, very valuable antique diamond brooch the bridegroom's mother had lent the bride to wear on her great day. Two little flower girls had been chosen, adorable in cream silk and cascades of tulle with long ribbons in their hair, and there were four bridesmaids in all, to match the bridegroom's tall, handsome attendants: the three cousins of the bride, Violette, Lilli and Rose, and, the fourth and chief bridesmaid, the beautiful sister of the bridegroom— Alexandra Radcliffe.

The bridesmaids, all blessed with perfect figures, wore elegant satin gowns cut like slips, which clung to the hip then fell to the floor in softly draped folds. The bride had proposed dawn shades—silver-grey, palest golden pearl, a beautiful blueish pink, and the softest amethyst. The bridesmaids, at first caught a little by surprise, had been thrilled with the finished gowns. It was the chief bridesmaid, Alexandra, who had hunted up a beautiful array of long vintage necklaces that lent additional glamour to the deep V of their gowns. All wore drop earrings of lustrous Tahitian pearls—a gift from the bride-groom—the iridescent colours of the pearls harmonised wonderfully with the particularly beautiful shades of their gowns.

When the moment came for the radiant bride to put back her veil and face her bridegroom, resplendent in his wedding finery of a grey morning suit, tears sprang to the eyes of every woman in the chapel and, it had to be said, quite a few of the men. The bride's uncle, Charles Denby, was even seen to discreetly blow his nose on a snowy white handkerchief.

It was that kind of wedding. Visually exquisite, tender and immensely moving. The love bride and groom felt for each other was so palpable it rayed over the assembly like a glorious heaven-sent light. Everyone in the chapel later swore they had felt the power of the ceremony, the utter seriousness of the vows. This was a couple who were in an enviable state of grace. Their union would bring even greater things to the Valley.

"Do you, Alana Maree Callaghan, take this man, Guy Balfour Radcliffe…"

Alana had thought in all the emotion of the moment her voice might fail her when the time came for her to say *I do*. But it emerged with the sweet clarity of her pure loving heart.

Finally the ceremony was over, and Guy—her wonderful Guy, her *prince*—took her in his arms.

"I adore you," Guy whispered emotionally against his wife's softly yielding mouth. "My wife—my beautiful Alana." Overwhelming happiness shone from his brilliant dark eyes.

"I adore *you,* Guy—my husband," she whispered back, thinking she was utterly blessed.

Together they turned as man and wife to face the beaming congregation. Immediately the organ, tuned to perfect pitch, sprang into rich, triumphant life. It filled the flower-decked chapel with the exuberant strains of the "Wedding March." Not to be outdone, sunlight chose that moment to pour like a benediction through the tall stained glass windows of the west wall of the chapel, creating a magical kaleidoscope of colour that caught the bride's veil and bathed it in jewelled lights.

An audible wave of delight swept through the chapel. Surely that was a good omen for the future?

Joyously, the beautiful bridesmaids followed after them. Alexandra was thinking it wouldn't be long before her own wedding day. Out of deference to Guy, his position, and all that he had achieved for the Valley, she and Kieran had decided they would wait until after he and Alana had celebrated their great day. Kieran had always scoffed at weddings in the past, but today she had caught his eye too many times to ever let him get away with that again. He had been as moved as she was, both of them touched by the power of love.

As the bridegroom's mother was heard to murmur to an elderly relative, swathed in lavender with pearls, "I simply can't imagine a more perfect wedding!"

"And Sidonie, dearest," the smile-wreathed relative responded, "their happiness has just begun."

* * * * *

Look out for Linc's story, coming soon!

Turn the page for a sneak preview of
AFTERSHOCK, *a new anthology*
featuring New York Times *bestselling author*
Sharon Sala.

Available October 2008.

n●cturne™

Dramatic and sensual tales of paranormal romance.

Chapter 1

October
New York City

Nicole Masters was sitting cross-legged on her sofa while a cold autumn rain peppered the windows of her fourth-floor apartment. She was poking at the ice cream in her bowl and trying not to be in a mood.

Six weeks ago, a simple trip to her neighborhood pharmacy had turned into a nightmare. She'd walked into the middle of a robbery. She never even saw the man who shot her in the head and left her for dead. She'd survived, but some of her senses had not. She was dealing with short-term memory loss and a tendency to stagger. Even though she'd been told the problems were most likely temporary, she waged a daily battle with depression.

Her parents had been killed in a car wreck when she was twenty-one. And except for a few friends—and most recently her boyfriend, Dominic Tucci, who lived in the apartment right above hers, she was alone. Her doctor kept reminding her that she should be grateful to be alive, and on one level she knew he was right. But he wasn't living in her shoes.

If she'd been anywhere else but at that pharmacy when the robbery happened, she wouldn't have died twice on the way to the hospital. Instead of being grateful that she'd survived, she couldn't stop thinking of what she'd lost.

But that wasn't the end of her troubles. On top of everything else, something strange was happening inside her head. She'd begun to hear odd things: sounds, not voices—at least, she didn't think it was voices. It was more like the distant noise of rapids—a rush of wind and water inside her head that, when it came, blocked out everything around her. It didn't happen often, but when it did, it was frightening, and it was driving her crazy.

The blank moments, which is what she called them, even had a rhythm. First there came that sound, then a cold sweat, then panic with no reason. Part of her feared it was the beginning of an emotional breakdown. And part of her feared it wasn't—that it was going to turn out to be a permanent souvenir of her resurrection.

Frustrated with herself and the situation as it stood, she upped the sound on the TV remote. But instead of *Wheel of Fortune,* an announcer broke in with a special bulletin.

"This just in. Police are on the scene of a kidnapping that occurred only hours ago at The Dakota. Molly Dane, the six-year-old daughter of one of Hollywood's blockbuster stars, Lyla Dane, was taken by force from the family apartment. At this time they have yet to receive a ransom demand. The housekeeper was seriously injured during the abduction, and is, at the present time, in surgery. Police are hoping to be able to talk to her once she regains consciousness. In the meantime, we are going now to a press conference with Lyla Dane."

Horrified, Nicole stilled as the cameras went live to where the actress was speaking before a bank of microphones. The shock and terror in Lyla Dane's voice were physically painful to watch. But even though Nicole kept upping the volume, the sound continued to fade.

Just when she was beginning to think something was wrong with her set, the broadcast suddenly switched from the Dane press conference to what appeared to be footage of the kidnapping, beginning with footage from inside the apartment.

When the front door suddenly flew back against the wall and four men rushed in, Nicole gasped. Horrified, she quickly realized that this must have been caught on a security camera inside the Dane apartment.

As Nicole continued to watch, a small Asian woman, who she guessed was the maid, rushed forward in an effort to keep them out. When one of the men hit her in the face with his gun, Nicole moaned. The violence was too reminiscent of what she'd lived through. Sick to her stomach, she fisted her hands against her belly, wishing it was over, but unable to tear her gaze away.

When the maid dropped to the carpet, the same man followed with a vicious kick to the little woman's midsection that lifted her off the floor.

"Oh, my God," Nicole said. When blood began to pool beneath the maid's head, she started to cry.

As the tape played on, the four men split up in different directions. The camera caught one running down a long marble hallway, then disappearing into a room. Moments later he reappeared, carrying a little girl, who Nicole assumed was Molly Dane. The child was wearing a pair of red pants and a white turtleneck sweater, and her hair was partially blocking her abductor's face as he carried her down the hall. She was kicking and screaming in his arms, and when he slapped her, it elicited an agonized scream that brought the other three running. Nicole watched in horror as one of them ran up and put his hand over Molly's face. Seconds later, she went limp.

One moment they were in the foyer, then they were gone.

Nicole jumped to her feet, then staggered drunkenly. The bowl of ice cream she'd absentmindedly placed in her lap shattered at her feet, splattering glass and melting ice cream everywhere.

The picture on the screen abruptly switched from the kidnapping to what Nicole assumed was a rerun of Lyla Dane's plea for her daughter's safe return, but she was numb.

Before she could think what to do next, the doorbell rang. Startled by the unexpected sound, she shakily swiped at the tears and took a step forward. She didn't feel the glass shards piercing her feet until she took the second step. At that point, sharp pains shot through her foot. She gasped, then looked down in confusion. Her legs looked as if she'd been running through mud, and she was standing in broken glass and ice cream, while a thin ribbon of blood seeped out from beneath her toes.

"Oh, no," Nicole mumbled, then stifled a second moan of pain.

The doorbell rang again. She shivered, then clutched her head in confusion.

"Just a minute!" she yelled, then tried to sidestep the rest of the debris as she hobbled to the door.

When she looked through the peephole in the door, she didn't know whether to be relieved or regretful.

It was Dominic, and as usual, she was a mess.

Nicole smiled a little self-consciously as she opened the door to let him in. "I just don't know what's happening to me. I think I'm losing my mind."

"Hey, don't talk about my woman like that."

Nicole rode the surge of delight his words brought. "So I'm still your woman?"

Dominic lowered his head.
Their lips met.
The kiss proceeded.
Slowly.
Thoroughly.

* * * * *

Be sure to look for the AFTERSHOCK *anthology*
next month, as well as other exciting paranormal stories
from Silhouette Nocturne.
Available in October wherever books are sold.

Harlequin® Historical
Historical Romantic Adventure!

HALLOWE'EN HUSBANDS

With three fantastic stories by

Lisa Plumley
Denise Lynn
Christine Merrill

Don't miss these unforgettable
stories about three women who
experience the mysterious
happenings of Allhallows Eve
and come to discover that finding
true love on this eerie day is not
so scary after all.

Look for
HALLOWE'EN HUSBANDS

Available October
wherever books are sold.

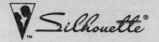

Romantic
SUSPENSE

Sparked by Danger,
Fueled by Passion.

USA TODAY bestselling author

Merline Lovelace

Undercover Wife

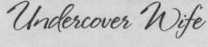

Secret agent Mike Callahan, code name Hawkeye,
objects when he's paired with sophisticated
Gillian Ridgeway on a dangerous spy mission
to Hong Kong. Gillian has secretly been in love
with him for years, but Hawk is an overprotective
man with a wounded past that threatens to
resurface. Now the two must put their lives—
and hearts—at risk for each other.

Available October wherever books are sold.

REQUEST YOUR FREE BOOKS!
2 FREE NOVELS PLUS 2
FREE GIFTS!

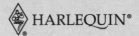

HARLEQUIN®

American ★ Romance®

HOLLY JACOBS
Once Upon a Thanksgiving

AMERICAN DADS

Single mom Samantha Williams has work, four kids and is even volunteering for the school's Thanksgiving pageant. Her full life gets busier when Harry Remington takes over as interim principal. Will he say goodbye at the end of his term in December…or can Samantha give him the best reason to stay?

Available October 2008 wherever books are sold.

LOVE, HOME & HAPPINESS

www.eHarlequin.com   HAR75236